P9-DFZ-368

"I want to be happy. Is that too much to ask?

"To just have one moment of unfettered joy without worrying where the next threat is coming from." Macie set her hand over his chest. "To feel something real and honest and exciting. I know it can't last forever. I know it's stupid when I'm stuck in the middle of a case, but I want—"

Riggs captured her mouth with his.

The momentum maneuvered her back into the wall riddled with bullet holes. Her hands fisted in his collar, pulling him closer, and his heart rate rocketed to keep up with the desire pulsing through his veins. Heat speared down his spine and into his gut so fast he had to catch his breath. Staring down at her, he tried to gauge her reaction. "Is that exciting enough for you?"

"I'm not sure." A smile tugged at one corner of her mouth. "Let's try it again."

DEAD AGAIN

———

NICHOLE SEVERN

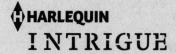

If you purchased this book without a cover you should be aware
that this book is stolen property. It was reported as "unsold and
destroyed" to the publisher, and neither the author nor the
publisher has received any payment for this "stripped book."

For the Harlequin Intrigue authors:
You inspire me on a daily basis.
Keep writing.

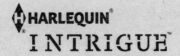

INTRIGUE™

Recycling programs
for this product may
not exist in your area.

ISBN-13: 978-1-335-58266-9

Dead Again

Copyright © 2023 by Natascha Jaffa

All rights reserved. No part of this book may be used or reproduced in
any manner whatsoever without written permission except in the case of
brief quotations embodied in critical articles and reviews.

This is a work of fiction. Names, characters, places and incidents
are either the product of the author's imagination or are used fictitiously.
Any resemblance to actual persons, living or dead, businesses,
companies, events or locales is entirely coincidental.

For questions and comments about the quality of this book,
please contact us at CustomerService@Harlequin.com.

Harlequin Enterprises ULC
22 Adelaide St. West, 41st Floor
Toronto, Ontario M5H 4E3, Canada
www.Harlequin.com

Printed in U.S.A.

Nichole Severn writes explosive romantic suspense with strong heroines, heroes who dare challenge them and a hell of a lot of guns. She resides with her very supportive and patient husband, as well as her demon spawn, in Utah. When she's not writing, she's constantly injuring herself running, rock climbing, practicing yoga and snowboarding. She loves hearing from readers through her website, www.nicholesevern.com, and on Facebook at nicholesevern.

Books by Nichole Severn

Harlequin Intrigue

Defenders of Battle Mountain

Grave Danger
Dead Giveaway
Dead on Arrival
Presumed Dead
Over Her Dead Body
Dead Again

A Marshal Law Novel

The Fugitive
The Witness
The Prosecutor
The Suspect

Blackhawk Security

Rules in Blackmail
Rules in Rescue
Rules in Deceit
Rules in Defiance
Caught in the Crossfire
The Line of Duty

Visit the Author Profile page at Harlequin.com.

CAST OF CHARACTERS

Macie Barclay—The Battle Mountain PD dispatcher has spent twenty-five years on the run and trying to solve a cold case on her own. But coming face-to-face with the childhood sweetheart she left behind wasn't the plan.

Riggs Karig—His mentor's death comes with confronting the woman he hasn't been able to forget. Macie is the only witness who remembers what happened the night their friend was murdered, and as a killer turns desperate, Riggs will do anything to make sure he doesn't lose Macie a second time.

Kevin Becker—The investigating detective assigned to the Hazel McAdams case and Riggs's mentor. Now he's in Battle Mountain...found dead with Macie's information in his pocket.

Hazel McAdams—Riggs's and Macie's best friend, found murdered twenty-five years ago.

Weston Ford—The only concern of Battle Mountain's police chief is keeping his town and his officers safe. No matter the cost.

Chapter One

Macie Barclay was leaving Battle Mountain.

And she wasn't ever coming back.

It didn't take a tarot reading or a lunar eclipse to tell her things were only going to get worse. Serial killers, bombers, psychopaths out for revenge and now crimes connected to cartels? Nope. She was out of here just as soon as she had everything packed. "Okay. What else?"

She shoved a few more dresses into her already bulging duffel bag and went to the bathroom to see what she'd left behind. She wouldn't be able to take all her things, but she'd done this before. Keep what was important, leave the rest.

It was too bad. She'd really loved this place. The town, too. Her entire house had been built around a one-hundred-year-old tree. Everyone in the police department had joked about her tree house, but this had been the one place she'd actually felt she belonged. Connected. Free to be herself without shame or judgment. Not the woman she'd created all those years ago. Not Macie Barclay. The real her. Her own scoff punctured through the trill of birds outside as she caught her reflection in the mirror over the sink. "You've been lying to yourself for so long, you don't even remember who that girl is anymore."

Macie closed her eyes, taking in the feel of the cool breeze through the window, the smell of the wood that made up these walls. She knew every inch of this house. From the claw-foot tub to the crack in the countertop downstairs in the kitchen. It'd seemed perfect. It'd felt like it was hers.

Macie forced her head back into the moment. Wouldn't do any good to sit around and feel sorry for herself. She'd make the next place perfect, too. No matter where that was.

Finished packing her clothes and toiletries, she headed back to the closet tucked away in the loft she'd used as a bedroom for the past six years. Hangers slid out of her way easily as she reached for the bifold shutters she'd installed at the back.

Anyone who'd come through this place had questioned her taste in decor, especially inside a closet nobody would see, but she'd put them in for a reason. She tugged at the right shutter and swung it wide. The photos and sticky notes she'd taped inside fluttered with the movement. Everything—crime scene photos she'd paid a former cop from Albuquerque PD to get for her, the autopsy report filed by a medical examiner who'd since been charged with corruption, notes of possible witnesses and family members to interview—it all had a place. Even one wrong placement could undo twenty-five years' worth of work.

Good thing she'd looked at this makeshift murder board a thousand times. She'd have no problem reassembling it wherever she ended up but unpocketed her phone and took a photo of the board in case. If anything happened, she could recreate any piece of the puzzle.

She peeled and untacked each piece of evidence she'd gathered since the day she'd left Albuquerque. No one would ever know why she'd joined Battle Mountain's police department as a dispatcher. Or why she'd run from New Mexico. And that was how it'd have to stay. There wouldn't be any goodbyes. No housewarming parties when she got to where she was going or help moving from the local church group. No home-cooked meals from Karie Ford out at the ranch or arguments with the pigheaded second-in-command, Easton Ford. Her heart hurt. A cold case was all she had left. And wasn't that just pathetic?

Macie outlined a photo that hadn't been included in the police's case file with the pad of her thumb. A photo taken of three toothy ten-year-olds standing in front of a bright yellow-and-red hot-air balloon half inflated before the festival. Her fiery hair stood out the most, but Hazel had been beautiful in her own right. That perfect smile—even with one of her eye-teeth missing—had blown away anyone who came in contact with her. Especially Riggs, the other kid in the picture. Right up until Hazel had been murdered. "I gave you my word."

Macie tucked scrawling notes, photos and reports into a file folder and slipped it into her messenger bag. This was it. She scanned the remains of the house. Everything she cared about was in that duffel bag on the bed, but the people she'd gotten to know—the friends she'd made—they all had to stay here. Live their lives. Be happy. Find a way to survive.

She just couldn't do it with them anymore. It was too dangerous. Macie Barclay had been a good name while she'd been here, but that wasn't her anymore. She shouldered her bag and zipped the bag closed. She didn't know where she'd end up tonight. It didn't matter. As long as it wasn't here.

Her keys trilled in her hand as she hauled her belongings off the bed and down the stairs. She'd done all the dishes, wiped down any surface that might hold her fingerprints and cleaned out the refrigerator. She worked with an entire department of cops. She had no doubt every one of them would spend the next few weeks trying to find her, but sooner or later, they'd give up. If they came looking for her, they wouldn't have the slightest idea of where to start, and her heart shuddered at the idea that Chief Ford, Kendric, Isla, Alma, hell, even Easton had never really gotten the chance to know the real her. Never would. That was just how it needed to be.

She gazed up into the exposed rafters and set her hand against the thickest part of the tree climbing up through the roof. "You were exactly what I needed when I needed it." Her throat threatened to close on a sob. "Thank you. For everything."

Macie gripped the handle of her bag. "Time to go."

She swung the front door open. And froze.

A man had raised his fist to knock, and a thread of fear slithered through her. He was handsome, devastatingly so, with piercing blue eyes that widened at the sight of her, but she'd been fooled by good looks before. And somehow, she knew him. Like they'd met before. "Macie Barclay?"

"Sorry. She doesn't live here anymore." Someone had come looking for her. Crap. She'd let herself get emotional about leaving, and it'd cost her. She had to get out of here. "Wish I could help, but I'm running late for my flight. If you'll excuse me." She wasn't flying. Her identity—no matter how many law enforcement databases she'd managed to alter with her access—wouldn't hold up against TSA.

Macie managed to get past him and closed the front door behind her, not bothering to lock it. Instead, she shoved her hand deep into the side pocket of her messenger bag and gripped the taser she'd started carrying out of necessity the past couple of years. She was halfway down the curving stairs before the mystery man tried again.

"Ava?" he asked.

She almost let go of her bag. No one had called her that since she'd been a girl running around with braids in her hair and as much sugar as she could haul in her pockets back in Albuquerque. Macie forced herself to keep moving. To get away. Nobody was supposed to find her here. She'd been careful, hadn't she? Moving every few years, changing her name, not letting the truth slip. What had she done wrong? "Sorry. I don't know anyone by that name. I hope you find what you're looking for."

"It's me. Riggs." He took a step down. Then another. "Riggs Karig. Do you remember me?"

Air crushed from her chest. She looked up at him from the bottom of the staircase. It hadn't been her imagination. The eyes, the shape of his mouth, the note of concern in his voice. For a moment, she saw her childhood best friend in the man he'd become, and her plan faded to the back of her mind. His five-o'clock shadow accentuated the sleepiness under his eyes. He hadn't changed much. Neither had the permanent scowl etched into his expression. It was him. She could feel it. Beard growth matched the dirty blond of his hair. It'd been darker the last time she'd seen him. A button-down shirt, open at the neck, showed off thick tendons and bulky muscle. She'd never missed the opportunity to appreciate a good view.

Riggs. All grown up.

He took another step down. A flash of a badge peeked out from beneath his jacket, and in an instant, the memories were gone. All that was left was regret she hadn't packed faster. The taser felt lighter than it should have hidden in the side pocket of her bag. She switched it on. As much as she hated the idea of pegging someone with fifty thousand volts of electricity, one thing remained clear: if Riggs Karig could find her, so could anyone else. "I told you, you have the wrong woman."

Macie forced herself to keep moving toward her crappy four-door sedan. She tossed her duffel bag into the back seat and climbed behind the steering wheel.

Then suddenly Riggs was there. He was holding her door open, trying to keep her from leaving, but she started the car anyway. "Avalynn, please. I need your help."

He was the only one who could get away with calling her by her full name. Except her mother, and that'd only been when she'd gotten into trouble. So…a lot. Macie gripped the steering wheel, knowing she'd regret not closing the door on his hand and making a break for it. She'd never been able to resist his charm in the past. Why would twenty-five years change anything? She forced herself to take a deep breath. "Help you with what?"

Riggs dug for a piece of paper in his jacket and

handed it to her. It was a decoy. In the next second, cold steel latched around her wrist. He secured the other end of the handcuff to the steering wheel and took a step back as Macie tried to close the door on him. "You can start by explaining why my partner was found dead with your name and address in his pocket less than six hours ago."

HE'D FOUND HER. After all these years, he'd finally found her.

Detective Riggs Karig leaned one shoulder into the car, watching Ava squirm. And, damn, was she a sight to behold. Long legs flexing under some kind of billowy floral dress as she struggled, curses that would make a sailor blush falling from full lips and all that fire red hair he'd teased her about as a kid— she hadn't changed. Even her penchant for flashy earrings threatened to bring him right back to his ten-year-old self like no time had passed between them. Avalynn Davis—no, Macie Barclay—was exactly as he remembered.

And everything he wanted to forget.

"So what was the plan here, Detective?" Macie gripped her cuffed wrist and hauled herself back to test the steel, but they both knew she wasn't going anywhere. "Keep an innocent woman handcuffed to her car like some kind of pervert?"

Detective. She was trying to distance herself. Pretend they hadn't gone through the same nightmare back in Albuquerque or that she hadn't known he'd been head over heels for her. He'd searched the entire country for her once he'd gotten hold of the resources after the academy. All this time, she hadn't been more than a state away. Riggs scanned the trees around the property. Not just any property. A tree house. It'd been set in the middle of the San Juan Mountains. Exposed, and ridiculous, and exactly the kind of place he'd imagined she'd go. "You keep doing that, you're going to break your wrist."

"You almost sound like you care about the woman you stalked across an entire state and cuffed to a car." His warning didn't stop her. Instead, it seemed to egg her on. She leveraged a booted foot against the door's frame and tried again. The links between the cuffs actually groaned, but Riggs wasn't letting her get away that easily.

He presented the key. Crystal green eyes that'd put most algae to shame locked on the brass then shifted to him. He could almost read her mind, her thinking of all the ways to pry it from his hand. Thinking of how far she could run before he caught up. She was right. He couldn't leave her like this. Becker's body wasn't even cold yet. Riggs was on the clock to find out who'd put his mentor in a body bag in the first place. That was all that mattered. "I give you this, you answer my questions. Deal?"

The possibility of freedom seemed to take the wind out of her sails, but Riggs had been lied to his entire career. He didn't trust anyone. Especially not a woman who'd stayed on the run all these years. Macie nodded. "All right. I answer one question, you let me go. Make it count. Because you will never see me again."

A flood of questions rushed to the front of his mind. Why had she left him? What had she been running from all these years? Had she been the one to strangle Becker and leave him to die in an abandoned building in the most isolated town he'd stepped foot in? It all came down to the same need for as much information as possible. Personal friendships, childhood memories, old feelings—none of it mattered in a homicide investigation. "Why did my partner have your name and address in his pocket when he died?"

Macie set that penetrating gaze on him and leaned forward slightly. The movement angled her arm against her throat, and Riggs was suddenly reminded of another strangling he'd tried to forget. "I don't know."

"That's it? You don't know." No. There had to be something more here. Becker hadn't come to this blip on the map and tracked her down for nothing.

"I answered your question, Detective." She rattled the cuffs as though to make a point, but Riggs had no intention of letting her rabbit on him again. "I'll be going now."

Something else was going on here. As much as he had to entertain the idea she'd had something to do with Becker's death, Macie Barclay didn't act like a killer. Which meant something had spooked her. "What are you running from, huh? Why are you in such a rush to get out of Dodge?"

A scoff turned her attention out the windshield of her rusted-out car. "You detectives are all the same. All you do is lie. To suspects, to witnesses." She rattled the cuffs again. "To yourselves. It's any wonder you manage to close cases at all."

"Does that make you a witness, Avalynn, or a suspect?" he asked.

"We're through here." Faster than he thought possible, she twisted her hand over the cuffs, and they fell free. Macie handed them off to him as though she hadn't just pulled off the greatest magic trick known to man. "I believe these belong to you."

"How'd you do that?" Riggs had never seen anything like it. She just kept a handcuff key on hand? Why? In case she ever landed under arrest?

"I've got plenty of tricks up these sleeves you haven't even begun to imagine." Her voice dipped into dangerous territory, and a flash of the hell-raiser who'd always gotten herself into all kinds of trouble as a kid surfaced. "I'd say it was nice seeing you, but then I'd be lying. Goodbye, Detective."

She moved to close the driver's side door again, but Riggs couldn't help himself. He couldn't let her leave. "A good man is dead, Ava. A good detective, and for some reason, you were the last thought on his mind before he was strangled. You have to know something."

She didn't even seem to breathe at his plea, as though she were used to people coming to her for help all the time. "This is personal for you. The detective who was killed. Who was he?"

"It was Becker," he said. "You probably don't remember him, but he was the lead detective during—"

"I remember him." Her hand fell away from the key still lodged in the ignition. Already pale skin seemed to drain of the last evidence of color. "What is it you want from me?"

"Did Becker reach out to you? Do you know what he was doing in Battle Mountain?" He just needed something—anything—to make sense of this. Becker had been the best of the best. Yeah, the retired detective had put away dozens of violent criminals, even worked task forces centered around bringing down the cartels moving in on New Mexico, but none of them had made a move like this. None of them had gone after a detective personally. If someone was making a move against the department, Riggs needed to know.

"No. I'm sorry for your loss, but Becker keeping his distance from me was probably for the best." Sincerity laced every word. She kept her hand on the door, ready to close it on him at any second. To walk away all over again and leave him behind. Ava— Macie—handed back the note he'd given her with her contact information sprawled in his own handwriting. It wasn't the original. As long as he was here in Battle Mountain, he didn't have jurisdiction to take the lead on this case, but he'd still handle the evidence as though he did. "Listen, it might not do any good, but you should check in with the interim chief. Battle Mountain PD is pretty good at this stuff."

Riggs's hand released her door. "Oh, yeah? Places consisting of seventeen hundred people see a lot of murder?"

"You obviously haven't been watching the news," she said. "You'd be surprised what a small town like this is willing to do to protect itself. Find Easton Ford. He'll help you."

What was that supposed to mean? Riggs stepped away from the car to give her room to leave. He believed her. Whatever Becker had wanted with Macie Barclay, the detective had taken to his grave, but the thought of letting her slip away again...

Movement caught his attention over the top of her car. From the trees about ten feet away. They were so thick, he couldn't see through to the other side. He hated that. All the greenery and shadows. Back in New Mexico, everything was flat, bare, exposed. Who knew how many threats waited here? His gut said it wasn't an animal, but he wasn't altogether familiar with this place, either. They were out in the middle of the woods. No neighbors for miles. Becker was dead, with Macie Barclay's contact information. He wasn't going to take any chances. "Ava, get out of the car."

"Stop calling me that like you know me, Detective. You don't, and I've humored you long enough." Macie pressed down on the brake pedal. "I can't stay here."

Riggs ripped open the door, grabbed her arm and dragged her from the car. They hit the dirt as one as a large knife cut through the air. A solid thud registered from overhead.

Ava—damn it, Macie—twisted her face up to the blade embedded deep into her tree house's wood staircase. "Is that a—"

"Stay down!" Riggs shoved to his feet. He took cover behind her vehicle and unholstered his weapon. Adrenaline threatened to tunnel his vision. He was met with nothing but pine trees and a breeze shaking through the wall of green, but the sick awareness of being watched didn't leave. No telling where the attacker had gone. But he wasn't going to stand around and wait for another attack. They needed to get out of here. Now. "Get to my truck. I'll cover you."

"I knew I should've left when I had the chance." Macie reached into the car and dragged a bag from the back seat. She stumbled forward, trying to keep her head down as she raced for his rental about ten yards away. "If I get stabbed in the back, I'm taking it out on you."

The low rumble of an engine broke through the

trees and grew faint. Smaller than a full-size engine. ATV, maybe. A hint of diesel filtered through the trees. Riggs kept his weapon aimed as he used the sleeve of his jacket to dislodge the blade. The metal whined upon release. He backed toward his truck, never once letting his sidearm dip. It wasn't just his life on the line. He had a duty to protect the woman who'd left him to rot in New Mexico alone.

He wedged himself into the driver's seat and holstered his weapon. "Hold this." He handed off the knife. After starting the truck, he fishtailed down the dirt road that'd brought him face-to-face with the friend he'd never thought he'd see again. "Someone killed my partner, and I think it's safe to say they just tried to kill you. So start talking, Macie, or whoever the hell you are. Who wants you dead?"

"That's funny." She pressed herself back into the seat. "I was about to ask you the same question, Detective Karig."

Chapter Two

It was happening all over again.

Battle Mountain had just barely started moving on from the last threat, lost its mayor and seen its police chief shot. Guess she didn't have to wonder what would come next. Riggs Karig had found her because someone had killed an Albuquerque homicide detective and now someone had thrown a freaking knife at her. Whether in warning or to actually hurt her, it didn't matter, but she knew what she had to do next.

She glanced toward the chief's office, expecting to find a warm familiar face staring at her through the blinds like Weston Ford so often did. He wasn't there, and her heart shuddered at the thought of not seeing the one person who didn't take her for an eccentric kook again. How long did it take for someone to recover from a bullet wound these days?

Macie checked if her bag was still stuffed under her desk. She'd had to leave her car back at the scene. She could walk out of this station right now—finish what she'd started—but she wouldn't get any farther than the end of Main Street. These particular boots were not made for walking.

It wouldn't be any use anyway. Riggs Karig would find her again. While she didn't know him personally anymore, collecting information and uncovering answers was in his and every other police officer's nature. And, whether she wanted to admit it or not, she was now part of a mystery he wanted to solve.

Interesting spot to be. She'd spent twenty-five years trying to melt into the background and avoid putting down roots. This place had made her soft.

"Show me your hands and turn around slowly." The definitive human-made click of a gun loading reached her ears.

Her insides lit up at the sound of the voice behind her. She did as she was instructed, raising her hands as high as her shoulders. Macie spun in her chair at the front of the station—slowly, of course—to find enormous blue eyes and the most beautiful wide gap-toothed smile. "You've got me, Officer Dwyer. I stole the cookie from the cookie jar. Would it help if I apologized?"

"Hand it over, scum." Penny Dwyer stretched one hand out, the other busy making the shape of a gun with her index finger and thumb. Her parents wouldn't let her have a toy gun considering what they did for a living. Probably the right choice, but it wouldn't stop the chaotic and vibrant four-year-old from following in their footsteps. "Swowly."

"Scum? That's harsh. Does your mom know you talk like that?" Macie made a big production of following along because honestly, Penny's visits were the only part of her day that didn't remind her of all the evil outside those double doors. Instead, she stood for the innocence of a childhood Macie had never had. "Okay. Okay. I'm just going to reach into my desk."

Macie gripped the item she'd left planted in her desk for over a week, waiting for this exact moment. "Here you go, Officer."

She made quick work of aiming the water gun at Penny and pulled the trigger. A shriek of glee and surprise filled the police station as Macie pursued the girl down the hall. Water spattered between Penny's shoulder blades and sent her running faster to the break room. "That's what you get, copper. You'll never get your hands on those cookies!"

The chief's door swung open. Riggs set himself dead center in her path. Macie's boots slipped against wet tile, and she flattened into the detective's chest. Hard muscle, coupled with strong hands, flexed against her to keep her upright. Seemed the little boy who'd followed her around as a kid had done some growing up since she'd left Albuquerque. A flash of a yellow shirt and the trail of laughter disappeared around the corner. "Dang it. You let her get away."

"Does this department usually have squirt gun wars in the middle of the day?" Riggs didn't seem too impressed with the way they did things around here, but Macie wasn't too overly concerned with his opinions. He'd dropped into her world. Not the other way around, and he wasn't staying. Then again, neither was she.

"Nerf gun wars, too. If we can manage to fit them into our busy schedule," she said.

Easton Ford stepped free from the chief's office. As interim chief of police, he had every right to sit behind that desk, even if Macie didn't like it. After his brother, Weston—Battle Mountain's true chief—had been shot a few days ago, someone had to step in. She supposed the former Green Beret was the best choice considering what little experience the rest of the officers in this office held. Easton had at least grown up here, was invested in the town and its people, especially its veterans. He'd even built a recovery center for them out at his family's ranch, Whispering Pines. It was where vets suffering with all manner of mental and physical health issues could go to feel safe and get the help they needed. Including Easton's fiancée, Genevieve. The Alamosa district attorney wasn't a vet, but she was a survivor, and her physical therapy at the ranch would be the only chance she'd get to walk again after she'd been grievously injured and confined to a wheelchair. "Detective Karig here was just filling me in. The body we recovered in one of the fire-damaged buildings this morning now has a name. Kevin Becker. Our coroner is up to her ears working with the military to sort through some bodies that dropped in town during a previous case, but she'll take good care of your friend. I give you my word."

"I appreciate that." Riggs shook Easton's hand. He was proving to have a solid poker face. Macie couldn't read his intentions or what he planned on doing next. Decades of sun exposure had created drought patches on his face, but that penetrating gaze remained clear, keen and probing. Not so quick with a smile. Direct, with a trustworthy face. He also filled out those jeans like he'd been born to them, and she couldn't deny he looked good. No wedding ring, though. Local girls would eat him alive.

"Great. Now you can go back where you came from." Macie set one hand at the small of his back—a very nice shape, if she had to say so herself—and maneuvered him down the hall toward the front of the station. He played along, but Macie had no doubt he could set her on her behind in one quick move. "So nice catching up with you. I'm sure you have better things to do than hang around Battle Mountain. Ford #2 will keep in touch about the investigation and let you know if we find anything. Bye-bye. Safe travels. Get out."

"Ford #2?" Riggs cast a glance back toward Easton.

"He's not going anywhere, Macie." Easton's voice

filled the station. Harsher than normal. She turned back to see him hefting her overnight bag from beneath her desk, and her lungs seized. He set it on the second level of her double-height desk but didn't move to open it. Her entire life was in that bag. "And neither are you."

Her hand fell from Riggs's back. Easton didn't have that authority. "What are you saying?"

Her temporary boss rounded her desk, before stopping short in what they'd lovingly called the lobby of the station. "I'm saying the detective told me everything while you were playing cops and robbers."

"Everything?" Her throat dried.

"You were leaving, weren't you?" Easton settled his massive body against the front desk, and irritation stupidly burned through her. It wasn't her desk anymore. She'd given it up to whoever BMPD decided to hire to dispatch next. "For good. Without a word to anyone."

"Do you blame me?" Awareness prickled between her shoulder blades as she became the center of attention. Right where she didn't want to be. "I'm not sure if you've noticed, but it seems every week we've got ourselves a new serial killer or arsonist to contend with. I didn't want to spend the years I have left being told my friends are dying off. Not including you, of course."

Easton's scoff broke the tension in his jaw. "Like you were informed of Hazel McAdams's death?"

The slap of shock took her retort out of her mouth. Rage unlike anything she'd felt before charged through her chest, and she turned on Riggs. "You had no right."

"He needed to know." Riggs didn't even bother to look sorry. "My partner was strangled to death less than a block from here, Macie. Protecting your feelings isn't high on my priority list. So, yeah, I told him. Because I'm not going to keep intel that could help me catch who did it from local police. Besides, aren't you the one who told me to come here? That this department was pretty good at these kinds of things?"

This wasn't happening.

"I talked to the Albuquerque PD captain that oversaw Kevin Becker for most of his career. He didn't have any idea why the detective would've come to Battle Mountain. But he's given Detective Karig permission to aid our investigation, and we're lucky to have him." Easton moved away from her desk, heading back to the office he'd taken over. "Oh, one more thing. Given the victim was found with your address on him, coupled with the attack at your home, Mace, I've asked Detective Karig to keep an eye on you for the duration of the case while we focus on the knife you recovered earlier." Amusement cracked through

Easton Ford's controlled expression. "From what I've heard, I'm sure you two will get along swimmingly."

"You've assigned me a babysitter?" Her and Easton's rivalry, their insults and her insubordination—it'd all been one big joke over the years, but this crossed a line. Macie wanted nothing more than to put a curse on him then, but she'd only started learning about ceremonial witchcraft a few weeks ago. "I knew there was a reason I didn't like you."

"And you can keep on not liking me as long as you're alive. I'm looking forward to it." Easton retreated to his office and closed the door. End of discussion.

"Guess it's you and me, Red." Riggs took up space in her peripheral vision.

"Don't get any bright ideas, Detective." It'd take a few hours to get the annoyance out of her system, but apparently, she didn't have any other place to be. "It's just temporary."

Right?

"If you say so." Riggs rubbed his hands together as though he was about to get a grip on a project he'd been looking forward to. "Where to?"

He wanted answers? Fine. She'd close this case for him as fast as possible and get him the hell out of Battle Mountain. She wasn't police, but she'd been around them long enough to pick up some skills. "Back to my house. Assuming your partner's killer threw that knife at us, we should try to retrace his steps."

"That's where I'd start, too," he said.

She buried the wave of pride at his words and headed for her desk to collect her bag.

Penny shot up from behind.

Macie's surprise was cut short as a beam of freezing water splashed into her face.

"I DON'T THINK I've heard anyone scream as loud as you did back there." Riggs couldn't help himself. It wasn't every day he got to see the wind taken out of the sails of a woman hell-bent on making everyone else question their sanity. "Your makeup smeared a bit under your eyes. I think I have a towel in the back seat if you want to try to get it off."

"So glad my misery could make your day a little better." Macie didn't move. Didn't even seem to breathe. It was hard to compare the carefree thrill seeker he'd known as a kid to the woman in the passenger seat. She wasn't anything he'd expected and kind of a pain in the ass but entertaining at the same time. "And I'm fine. Thank you."

The truck bumped and skidded up the same dirt road he'd traveled this morning. He hadn't known what waited at the end, but he sure as hell hadn't planned for Macie. Her self-awareness and moodiness alone outshined any memories of the past, leaving nothing but curiosity. She'd become a police dispatcher, worked with law enforcement and watched every single officer in that department risk their lives for this town. Why? Riggs tightened his grip on the steering wheel to be ready for the tires to slip out from under them. "You don't seem to like the interim chief much. I take it there's some history there."

"What gave it away?" She stared out the passenger window as though convinced just looking at him would give away every secret she'd ever held on to. He was a good detective, but he wasn't that good.

"Calling him Ford #2 was a bit of a hint." It'd taken every ounce of control he had not to laugh at it, either. Other than the straight up insubordination, Macie was proving to be one of a kind. Like this place. He hadn't come across that in a while.

"You were asked to keep me alive, Detective. Not get to know me," she said. "Just because you're my babysitter, doesn't mean we have to be friends."

"Fair enough, but to be clear, none of this was my idea." Jagged cliffs and peaks held on to the remnants of winter around them but still managed to produce entire layers of greenery. If he was being honest with himself, he hated this place. It was nothing like New Mexico. There was a weakness here that came with relying on shade and protective cliffs. Back home, things had to survive. A place like this didn't present a challenge in the least. He couldn't help make the internal comparison. He'd known from the time he'd been ten years old that he wanted to be a detective and help solve crimes, but with Becker out of the picture… He wasn't sure what else was left for him to do. He needed something more. Something to give him that spark that'd died over the past few years. "Seems Ford #2 genuinely cares about what happens to the people in his department. I told him my theory. He came up with the protection gig."

"Yeah, then what's your theory?" she asked.

Riggs's gut clenched. "That Becker's strangling wasn't random. I think he found something. He had your address for a reason. He could've been looking for you because you're connected to the McAdams case, and the killer followed him." Of course, there were a lot of other variables, but his instincts said he'd hit the mark. No one had been arrested in the murder of Hazel McAdams. Someone had been trying to stop Becker from getting to the truth. And they'd succeeded. "But you're right. We don't need to be friends. I was just trying to make the drive less awkward."

Silence pressed in through the truck cabin.

"He's too practical." Macie rubbed her palms against her knees and turned her attention out the windshield. "Easton. It works for him, and a big part of why this town is still on the map is because of him. I know that. He was military. There wasn't a whole lot of room for joking around and fun, and after what he went through to land him his discharge, I can see why he takes everything so seriously. There are lives at risk when he's working a case. He knows the best way to take down a threat and protect the people of this town, but life is about more than getting the job done at the end of the day." She half turned toward him, the sourness etched into her expression draining with every word. It was a sight to behold. "It's about finding meaning along the way."

Meaning. A flash of memory took him by surprise. Hazel and Ava—Macie—jumping over and falling into Las Huertas Creek on a school field trip up the mountain. They'd gotten soaked to the bone, but they'd kept the biggest smiles on their faces. Even when the teacher had chided them. It was that same creek where Becker and a couple police K9 units had found Hazel after her disappearance—an area they'd searched before but found nothing. The killer had returned the body to the scene of her abduction. "Our line of work doesn't allow for much meaning when we have to face the worst humankind has to offer."

"You're right." Macie's voice softened. "But it can't be all bad either, can it? Otherwise, what's the point?"

He didn't have an answer to that. Riggs maneuvered the truck onto another road, giving them a straight shot to her tree house. Which was a bit out of the box itself. What kind of woman lived in an actual tree house? Macie. That was who. Even as a kid, she'd always leaned into the unique. Never stopped learning something new. Like there was a piece of her missing, and she was trying to fill the gap. It was one of the reasons he'd liked her so much. He'd wanted to see what else she'd uncover about the world. He'd wanted to see the brightness in her face as she taught him about it, too.

Riggs pulled the truck into the makeshift driveway he'd parked earlier. A Battle Mountain police cruiser waited across the property, but he didn't see any officers to accompany it.

"That's Alma's and Cree's," she said. "They'll be around here somewhere."

Hesitation had him reaching for Macie before she got out. Soft skin slid beneath his calluses, and if that wasn't the metaphor of the year, he didn't know what was. She hadn't seen the things he had, hadn't been hardened by the realities of the world. No. Instead, Macie Barclay had run from the hard things as soon as she could and never looked back. She got to pretend evil didn't sink into the cracks around them and take over. While he'd been left to deal with the consequences. "Let me take a look first. Just to be safe."

She settled back into her seat. Surprising. He'd expected her to fight tooth and nail and shout about her ability to protect herself if it came right down to it. But it was then he caught sight of the bag she'd been hauling to her car when they'd met this morning, now at her feet. He'd noted the tension in her shoulders when Easton Ford had set it on her desk back at the station. She was protective of it. No doubt. So maybe she was letting him take the lead to get ready to run again.

Riggs hit the dirt, taking his keys with him, and scanned the tree line. He felt more exposed out here than he did in the middle of a flat desert. Unfamiliar territory had always put him off-balance, but he'd trained to handle anything the job threw his way. His personal life was another matter.

Hand poised above his sidearm, he headed for Macie's car. The keys were still inside. With a quick glance back toward his truck, he collected them from the ignition. If her plan had been to accompany him back out here to collect her car and disappear for another twenty-five years, she'd be sorely disappointed.

A breeze shifted through the trees and tightened his nerves. An echo of the engine he'd heard after the attack stalled on the wind. He didn't have that same feeling of being watched that he'd had earlier. Probably just his imagination. Still, he didn't trust his instincts out here. Riggs pocketed her keys, laughing at the hot-pink *coffee, chocolate and me: some things are better rich* key chain. He headed back toward her. Knocking on the window, he then stepped back as she cracked the door. "I want to take a look inside. Make sure nothing is missing, if that's all right with you."

"Did you find anything that would tell you who tried to fillet us?" Macie climbed down from the truck, one long leg peeking out from the split in her dress. Patches of dust had stained the white background of bright flowers and stems, but she'd taken his tackle like a champ. Maybe she wasn't as delicate as he'd initially believed.

"Not yet." He had an idea, but he wasn't ready to make a statement. Considering the use of an ATV and how quickly the killer had escaped down this mountain, whoever killed Becker hadn't followed the detective from Albuquerque. He'd already been here. And he knew the area.

They headed up the grand staircase complete with an extra split in the wood. The door was already unlocked, but he recalled Macie hadn't locked it behind her when he'd confronted her the last time they were here. She'd been set on leaving in a hurry. And from his guess, never intended on coming back. No point in locking a place you're leaving when disappearing for good. She'd done the same thing to her house in New Mexico.

"Oh." Macie pulled up short in the doorway, but even from a few inches behind her, he saw the same thing she did. Absolute destruction. "I don't... I don't understand."

Riggs maneuvered past her, catching a lungful of sensual perfume that seemed to fit her perfectly. But it wasn't enough to diffuse the chaos around them. Broken dishes had been scattered across the wood floor, chairs overturned where the dining set was supposed to be. Chunks of wood splintered away from the tree the house had been built around, as though the killer had been looking for something.

"He must've come back after we drove away." Riggs didn't want to touch anything. Everything in this room could be considered evidence. "Searched for something to connect you to Becker."

Macie didn't follow the same protocols. She carved a path through the mess and headed straight upstairs.

"Macie, wait." He tried to grab her arm, but she was too fast. Determined.

She didn't answer, disappearing beyond the two-story banister separating a loft from downstairs. Shuffling registered from above, and Riggs couldn't help himself.

"Damn it." He waded through the remnants of her personal possessions as carefully as possible. Upstairs hadn't survived any more than the first floor. Pillows spilled their guts, the mattress had been shredded and Macie…just stood there. His heart gripped hard. While she'd intended to leave this house, he understood it'd be hard to come face-to-face with this alienating destruction. Riggs slowed his approach, taking in what looked like hinged window shutters installed at the back of an empty closet. "What was in here?"

She seemed to snap out of whatever thought she'd been stuck in and closed the closet doors. "Nothing."

Chapter Three

She hadn't lied to him.

Macie had emptied that closet a few minutes before he'd gotten to the house, but somehow the killer had known about it.

Or maybe he'd gotten lucky.

She didn't know. Either way, someone had caught on to what she'd been doing all these years. They'd broken into her home, gone through her things. She shouldn't care. She'd planned on leaving it all behind, but she couldn't dislodge the sense of violation. That house had been hers for six years. It'd been home longer than anywhere else. Was that how Detective Becker had found her? Had she made a mistake?

Riggs drove them down Main Street, heading back for the station. Last they checked, Alma Majors and Cree Gregson were still following the ATV tracks through the woods. They'd be out there until the sun went down. Waste of time. Macie already knew what they'd come back with. Nothing. In her experience, the killer would've found a way to disappear. Wasn't that how the past five murder cases in Battle Mountain had worked?

She studied residents enjoying the first real day of spring. Snow still capped the cliffs protecting the town from outsiders, but temperatures were on the rise. "Can we please stop for something to eat? My stomach doesn't feel good."

Heat spread through her as Riggs glanced in her direction. "No problem. Anything good around here?"

"The coffee shop is fine." She pointed out Caffeine and Carbs' new location a few doors down from the station. Normally, she would've gone to Greta's—Battle Mountain's oldest and authentically grimiest diner—but grease wouldn't cure what ailed her. She needed straight up caffeine to settle her nerves.

The detective angled into a parking spot, rounded the hood of the truck and waited. For her. The part of her that wasn't freaked out by a throwing knife and someone going through her house appreciated it, but Macie knew exactly what he was doing. It was what all of the reserve officers in the department had done when lives were at risk: followed orders. He was taking his protection detail seriously. Riggs walked beside her all the way to the door and held it open for her. "After you."

Macie headed straight for the counter, not even bothering to glance at the pastries in the baker's cases on either side. She'd tried not to feed her sweet tooth since she'd made herself sick eating so much candy as a kid. Unlike Isla Vachs, BMPD's newest recruit. Actually, she was surprised the former EMT wasn't already here for her daily hit of sugar and chocolate.

"Hey, Macie." Reagan Allen wiped his hands on a dishcloth from behind the counter. He'd been an institution in Battle Mountain since the day she'd rolled into town. The former competition pastry chef had gotten tired of the rat race and wanted something quiet. Too bad that hadn't really worked out for him considering his bakery had burned down with the help of an arsonist about nine months ago. Not to mention the forest fire on the outskirts of town and all the dead people turning up. No doubt he'd already heard about the one in the next building over. "Get you the usual?"

"No." Her voice shook more than she'd meant it to. Macie leveled her chin parallel to the floor. "Today, I want my unusual please."

Silence descended from the couple a few tables over.

"Hell, woman." Reagan dropped the towel on the counter. "You haven't ordered that since Easton Ford signed up with the department. You sure?"

"I know what I'm about, Reagan Allen. I'm not a child." She could handle the caffeine. No matter what anyone in this town believed.

"All right." The baker held his hands up in surrender. A bandage had been plastered along one side of his left one. Reagan was always trying new things in the bakery. It wasn't uncommon for him to catch a few burns a week. "One blonde roast coffee coming up."

"Am I missing something?" Riggs asked.

"No. I'm just thirsty." She'd forgotten he was there at all. Macie left her money on the counter as Reagan handed her the extra-large coffee. Heat soaked into her hands through the Styrofoam cup, like the contents were trying to be absorbed through her skin. Today she finally understood why people wished they could be hooked up to their coffee intravenously, but she'd do it the old-fashioned way.

Riggs ordered his drink. Something loaded with cream and sugar, plus a pastry. Whatever he did to keep in shape, it was obviously working.

"You're gonna want to watch her." Reagan tried to keep his voice down as he handed off Riggs's order, but noise carried in a place like this. "Last time she had one of those, police found her out in the middle of the woods in a sleeping bag with a bunch of stuffed animals tucked in tight. She didn't remember any of it."

Every muscle in her body tensed for the laugh, but it never came.

"Good to know." Riggs dropped a few coins into the tip jar. "Thanks for the coffee."

They left together, stepping out into the too bright sun and the slow mingling of townspeople conducting their own business in the middle of the week. But the tension was still there. "You're not going to ask me about what Reagan told you?"

"Why would I?" Riggs took a huge bite of his chocolate glazed donut like he'd never tasted anything so good. Looked like cops really did like their pastries. He followed it up quickly with a big sip of coffee. "Sounds like you weren't hurting anyone or destroying property. What you choose to do with stuffed animals in the middle of the woods is none of my business."

His tone said otherwise. "You're not even a little bit curious?"

"Like I said, it's got nothing to do with me." Heading down the street, he finished off his donut and tossed the wrapper into the garbage can on the way. "Tell me what happened to these buildings."

Macie had yet to take a shot of her overcaffeinated coffee, but her hands had somehow stopped shaking. She studied the back of Riggs's head, and a flash comparison to the boy she'd known superimposed over reality. He'd always been inquisitive, especially about things he didn't understand. The bizarre and unusual. Like the more knowledge he collected, the farther he could go. Literally and figuratively. But the crest on the badge around his neck said he hadn't gone far. He was Albuquerque born and bred. No amount of education was going to peel him from his hometown.

They stopped in front of one of the first buildings that'd been affected by the bombing at the station. "This was the fly shop. Lake San Cristobal isn't far from here. We get a lot of fishermen and tourists passing through who are looking for a taste of the outdoors. Some regulars. Well, we used to."

"What happened to it?" He surveyed the crumbling concrete structure. The roof had caved in as the resulting fire spread. Remnants of the front sign still clung to the edges, but there was nothing to save.

"There was a bomb." She could still feel the heat of it burning her from head to toe. If it hadn't been for Cree Gregson and his quick instincts, she would've been one of its victims. She was a dispatcher. She wasn't supposed to be caught in the danger. All these years, she'd expected the threat to come out of Battle Mountain. Turned out, this place wasn't the source after all. It'd followed her here. Just like the detective who'd been killed. "Nine months ago. An ATF agent had murdered her sister. She was doing everything she could to stop the department from catching her. Caused the forest fire, too."

"I noticed the burnt trees on the way in," he said. "This place has got a few scars, from the looks of it."

He had no idea.

Riggs walked along a little farther. "What about this one?"

"This was Caffeine and Carbs." This building looked like the others. Maybe a little worse for wear. Macie had no idea why the city hadn't bulldozed these already. Business owners didn't have the money to rebuild after insurance denied their claims, and Battle Mountain didn't have the funds to revitalize any of it. This town had started dying the moment the coal companies pulled out, and it was only getting worse with this new wave of crime. "Reagan's insurance didn't cover a rebuild, so he decided to take over one of the buildings that hadn't been as damaged. Started fresh."

"Becker was here. I don't know why. I don't even know how he found you and what the hell he was doing in this building." His voice dipped, solemn and pained. "It killed him to retire without having an answer to the one case that'd haunted him."

"Hazel's." Macie understood the feeling. It felt as though she'd put her entire life on hold for breadcrumbs when what she really needed was the whole loaf. She could only imagine how hard the detective who'd overseen the investigation had pushed all these years, but the trail had gone cold long before she'd left Albuquerque.

Hazel McAdams had been more of a sister than a best friend. They'd shared the same birthday and were hardly ever apart from kindergarten all the way through fifth grade. She wasn't sure when Riggs had joined their little band of merry hell-raisers, but he'd fit right in as though he'd always been there. Actually, she was pretty sure he'd had a crush on Hazel. Most people did. Hazel had been the city's sweetheart. Perfect in every way with a great big smile and gorgeous blond hair. As an only child, she'd gotten her parents' love with extravagant birthday parties and beautiful dress-ups. Teachers had given her extra gold stars. The girl could've done no wrong, in anyone's eyes.

But Hazel had made a mistake. One that'd cost her life.

Macie tried to keep the memories from encroaching on the moment. The police had spared no expense in the hunt. The entire city had been up in arms with volunteer searches, flyers, pleas in the paper and on the news. The McAdamses had offered a reward, but that'd only thinned the police force out there in the streets and woods by giving them empty leads to chase. Detective Becker had stuck with it, though. He'd been the one to find her three days later. This was her chance to make things right. To move on. "Was there anything he said to you? A lead or someone who came forward with new information?"

"Yeah. There was. I found his notes locked in the trunk of his car. From what I could tell, he'd gone back through the original file. I took a look at the crime scene photos and found a note he'd written on a Post-it. The same shoe tread could be found all over those woods. Like Hazel had run from her abductor. Police figured every child-sized imprint had come from her during a struggle with the killer, but he believed there were two sets of footprints in those woods. Same shoe. Two different sources." Riggs locked that penetrating gaze on her, his index finger extended at her from around his coffee cup. "According to Becker, Hazel wasn't alone the day she was killed."

"WHAT ARE YOU asking me, Detective?" Macie seemed to shut down right then. Those fish bait earrings of hers had a lot to say, though. They caught in her hair as wind cut down the street from the canyon and cliffs southward.

"You were there, weren't you?" He hadn't ever considered the possibility. The evidence had been straightforward. Identical shoe treads all across that mountain. One belonged to the killer—that much had been easily discernible, but the others... "The day Hazel was taken. The day she was killed. That's why Becker wanted to track you down. He must've remembered you two had been inseparable. You dressed alike, sometimes with the same earrings, same shirts. Did your hair the same way. And I remember those shoes, Macie. White-laced sneakers with hot-pink scales. You begged your parents for them for months because Hazel had ones just like them. You were so excited when you finally got them for your birthday."

She tossed her coffee—completely full—into the street bin. "I'm sorry you lost your partner. Really, I am. I don't know why Becker had my contact information in his pocket when he died or why he came here. I don't know who killed him, and I can't help you."

Riggs couldn't let her go. Not yet. He slipped his hand between her arm and rib cage, before pulling her into his chest. Her softness turned hard as she pressed against him. "I think you know more than you're letting on. I think you know exactly who killed my partner and why Becker wanted to find you, but you're either in denial this has anything to do with you, or you're hiding something from me."

Her bottom lip parted, but still, she didn't answer. Like she'd betray some kind of promise if she did.

"That's why you left, isn't it? Why one day I showed up at your house and the entire place had been cleared out." Riggs released his hold on her. All this time, he'd resented her for leaving him to deal with Hazel's death alone, for disappearing. What if he'd had it wrong? What if Hazel and Macie had been together that day? What if Hazel's killer had taken them both and nobody had known until she'd reported what'd happened to police? "I tried calling for days. I went by your house. Becker was there. I asked him if he knew anything about where you'd gone. He had no idea. One day you were there, and the next day you were gone." The truth set in. It sucker punched him harder than he'd expected. "I thought it was because you couldn't take staying in the same city where you'd lost your best friend, but you and your parents left because you thought Hazel's killer might come back for you. Didn't you?"

A line of tears welled in her eyes, but what little he knew of this new version of her told him Macie wasn't the kind of woman to let them fall. She backed away from him, out of reach. "That's quite a theory, Detective."

"It's not just a theory, is it?" He thought his past cases had emotionally wrung him dry from the inside out, but right then, his heart gripped hard in his chest. Twenty-five years on the run. Terrified. Alone. How had she survived? "You escaped him."

Macie cut her attention to a couple crossing the street. "We went back to that creek. You know, the one where Mrs. Reich took us for a field trip to study algae and insects in moving water that one time. We thought we could win the entire science fair if we were able to grow our own algae, but we figured it was like making sourdough bread. We needed a starter first, a sample. Stupid, I know, but we didn't know any better."

Her laugh died as wind howled down Main Street, rising to the obvious storm churning inside her.

"I don't know where he came from." Green eyes unlike anything he'd seen until he'd met her darkened as clouds blocked out the sun. "One second, we were throwing moss at each other, the next he was standing there."

Tension flooded through his neck and shoulders as though he could intervene on her behalf. "Did he talk to you?"

"He told us he was lost, then asked us if we knew the way back down the mountain. It all happened so fast I never got a good look at his face. He grabbed me from behind. I kicked and screamed, but he was so strong." She hugged her middle. "Hazel grabbed for a dead branch and hit him in the back to get him to let me go. Worked, too." Clarity spread across her expression. "He let me go, but he caught the branch Hazel was swinging and turned on her. I don't remember much after that."

"You must've gotten back down the mountain somehow. You made it home. Your parents are the ones who called the police, but they never mentioned you'd been with Hazel that day." Guilt had obviously been eating away at the sunshine inside of her since she'd left Albuquerque, but children weren't supposed to know how to fight off attackers. They were supposed to know how to jump rope, navigate puberty and do their schoolwork. They were supposed to believe in Santa Claus and fight with their siblings. Not full-grown men. What she'd been through… No ten-year-old should've had to face that, but there was something in her eyes that said she'd held herself responsible ever since. "Where did you go?"

"Canada, at first. It was the farthest my parents could get me while staying on the continent. We found an isolated plot of land in Newfoundland and acquired it to build a cabin," she said. "They're still there as far as I know."

He didn't understand. "What do you mean? You don't talk to them?"

"I mean I got tired of watching them check the doors and windows multiple times a night. I got tired of the weekly trips to the gun range and stashing our food like the end of the world was coming. I wasn't allowed to go to school. They didn't let themselves get to know anyone. They were suspicious of everyone. As long as I was there, they would've kept giving up their lives for me, and I couldn't take it. I knew sooner or later, they'd resent me for it," she said. "So I didn't give them the chance. When I turned seventeen, I told myself I would never let anyone else put themselves in danger for me, and I left."

He didn't know what to say to that, what to think. "Macie, I'm sure they were just happy you survived. They were doing what I wish all parents would do. Protecting you. What more could you have asked for?"

"I guess I'll never know." The tears were gone. In their place, defiance took control, and Macie was back to being the firecracker waiting to blow up in his face. "You can consider your babysitting duties fulfilled, Riggs. Now you know the truth. Both Hazel and Becker died because of me, and I'm not going to let anyone else make the same mistake. Including you." She swiped a strand of hair out of her face. His name sounded whole and compelling coming from her mouth, like it was some kind of lifeline, and he wanted nothing more than for her to latch on to it. "I hope you find who killed your partner. Becker deserved better. Don't try to find me again. Please."

He reached out again, hating himself for even trying as she flinched. "You can't run from this, Macie. Whoever did this… He's going to find you just like I did."

"I like my chances." They were back at his truck. Macie wrenched open his vehicle door. Lugging her duffel bag over her shoulder, she blocked her face from the incoming rain and headed down the street back toward the police station. Within seconds, the town's drainage system struggled with the amount of water, and he was completely soaked through, from head to toe.

She had a point. Anyone who'd tried to help her had turned up dead or on the run. He'd be stupid to follow after her now that he knew why Becker had come to Battle Mountain. He had another piece of the puzzle in place. By her own words, there wasn't anything else Macie Barclay could give him, but the thought of letting her go without a solid plan for her protection in place gutted him.

"Damn it." Macie was so determined to run, she'd

plow straight into a tree if she thought it'd get her out of here faster. Riggs jogged to catch up with her, tossing his coffee on the way. "You're not getting anywhere in this downpour. Your tree house is still a crime scene. You can't go back there. What are you going to do? Sleep in the station? The only beds they have are made of concrete and surrounded by steel bars."

"That's not your problem, Detective." She cut through the storm as though she'd done it a thousand times before. Which was a probability in a place like this. Lightning lit up the sky a split second before thunder shook the very ground he stood on. Hell. Had Battle Mountain opened a hell gate he didn't know about?

"You don't have to do this, Macie." He wasn't sure why he was petitioning for more time other than the simple fact that as long as she was with him, he would keep her alive. He could make up for not being there for Becker when his partner had needed him the most. "Help me. Please."

She turned on him. Water streaked down her high-boned cheeks and framed her chin. "Help you? Do what?"

"End this," he said.

"Did you not hear what I just said, Riggs? Anyone I get close to ends up dead or in some cabin in the middle of Canada. Even if I agreed to stay, I'm not a detective, Riggs." Macie glanced toward the station two doors down. He could see the wheels spinning in her head, see how much she wanted to walk away. But he couldn't do this without her. "I'm a dispatcher. I don't know the first thing about investigating a homicide."

"But you know this killer. You survived him." He held himself back from putting the cuffs on her again, to keep her from leaving a second time. Wouldn't do any good. For all he knew, she'd hidden handcuff keys in the seams of her dress. "Aren't you tired of running, Macie? Don't you want to finally feel safe? If we work together, if we put the bastard who killed our friends behind bars, you can be free. You can see your parents again. You can finally have a life."

Macie gave the station another longing look. "Don't make promises you can't keep."

Chapter Four

She'd lied to him.

About that day in the woods. She'd recalled the memories so many times, there wasn't anything she could do to keep them from haunting her. The secret she'd carried from that day forth wouldn't help find who'd killed his partner, and it wouldn't help catch the man who'd killed Hazel.

Its sole purpose was to punish her.

Riggs closed the door behind them, shutting out the storm. He shucked out of his jacket and ignited a lungful of something along the lines of spicy after-shave and earth in the enclosed space. It pricked at her senses. A perfect distraction from reality. "Make yourself at home."

She scanned the too-small room as she peeled her own jacket free from the dress suctioned to her skin. Single bed, a dresser topped with an old TV. No chairs. A door across the room led into the bathroom. No matter where she looked, brown reigned. In the carpet, the curtains, the wood paneling. Everything looked like it'd taken a flush down a toilet then come back up and spilled over every inch of the place.

Cindy's Motel hadn't been affected by the fires, serial killers, bombers or gunmen. It was the one spot in all of Battle Mountain that seemed safe, but the pressure in Macie's rib cage refused to relent. She squeezed the handle of her duffel bag tighter as the walls seemed to cave in. "Not sure where I can do that seeing as how the only place to sit is the bed."

He collected a backpack near the door and maneuvered past her on his way to the bathroom. Ridges and valleys of muscle across his back flexed under every move. "Is that you worrying about me sleeping on damp bedding tonight, or your way of talking yourself out of staying?"

Macie caught herself staring at the white T-shirt plastered to him like a second skin. Holy hell. The man had done more than a little growing up. He'd taken very good care of himself, indeed. "Both. I think." She couldn't really remember what he'd asked.

"You're going to want to close your mouth before that spider in the corner finds a new place to stay." He pointed overhead. That crooked smile she'd only gotten a taste of earlier made a full appearance a split second before he disappeared into the bathroom and closed the door. "I might have something you can change into. Get you out of that dress. Unless you're not staying."

Thunder crashed overhead and shook the cheap window at the back of the room as though to make a point. This storm had been waiting in the mountains for three days and was just the beginning of a series that hit every spring. Roads flooded, mudslides blocked entire passages and accidents increased. Unfortunately, she wasn't going anywhere until it passed.

Macie unshouldered her bag and set it on the bed. The canvas had protected most of what was inside. She wouldn't have to borrow any of Riggs's clothes. Sleeping arrangements, on the other hand, would be awkward. Flipping through her files, she ensured Easton Ford hadn't taken anything while he'd man-handled her bag back at the station. Nosy, no-good imposter. She took a cleansing breath, still picking up hints of spice. Everything was there. "You said Becker was your partner. He must've been close to sixty now."

"Sixty-three." Riggs's answer was nearly drowned under the patter of running water. The shower?

"How long were you partners for?" Macie took the opportunity to run through the rest of the room. Nothing in the dresser drawers. Seemed the detective traveled light. Preferred to be ready to go at a moment's notice. She liked that. She understood that. Closing the top dresser drawer, she moved to the nightstands with a glance toward the bathroom door. The motel Bible had seen better days, but it'd been dusted recently. No sign of a phone or laptop. Not even a charger. Riggs would have to keep in touch with his department. He must have taken them into the bathroom with him.

"Three years, but we've been friends longer." The door swung open, and a wall of steam escaped upward. "Can I help you find something?"

Macie slammed the nightstand drawer closed and straightened as fast as her upper body allowed. Not fast enough. He'd caught her snooping. She could see it in the amusement plastered across his gorgeous face. "Floss?"

"Floss." That single word told her everything she needed to know. He was a much better detective than she'd given him credit for. Riggs had lost his shirt, accentuating lean muscle, narrow hips and that little V thing men got when they worked out. He wadded and wrung the fabric stretched between his hands. "And the first place you thought to check for that was my nightstand?"

"I have sensitive teeth." Heat burned up her neck and into her face. He wasn't stupid. He knew exactly what she'd been doing, but he was giving her the benefit of the doubt for some reason. "It's genetic."

"Right. And is snooping through other people's personal belongings genetic, too, or does that come with the Macie Barclay package?" Riggs hung the shirt over his shoulder.

"Fine. You caught me. Okay? I was looking through your room to see what I could find out about you." What was a little spying between friends? "Hard to tell who's actually telling the truth these days. For all I know, you could be the one who killed your partner and were trying to hunt me down."

She regretted the words the moment they'd left her mouth.

The pain registered on his face, but Riggs hid it well. "Kevin Becker was the only person who ever gave a damn about me. My parents pretty much checked out after my brother came into the world. Becker saw what losing you and Hazel did. I was alone. I was scared I was next. He encouraged me to face my fears. When I joined the force, he taught me how to run an investigation, to stick with it and get my own answers. He's the reason I became a detective. Becker was a good investigator, but he was an even better man. I'd never have hurt him. Least of all to find you."

"I'm sorry. I didn't mean…" She wasn't sure what she'd meant, but one thing he'd said had stood out among the rest. Macie took a half step toward him. She didn't know why other than to make herself feel better about her accusation by offering some comfort, but she wasn't good at that, either. "You've been looking into Hazel's case all this time?"

"What else was I supposed to do? Pretend everything was normal. That you'd just show up at my doorstep one day, and you'd go back to being all I had?" He talked as though that'd been exactly as he'd done, and her heart hurt at the thought.

Of course, there'd been times she'd imagined that day playing out differently. That she'd been the one to stay behind and Hazel had made it out alive. That they'd both fought for each other. Maybe even grew up, became pop stars like they'd always imagined. That they'd fall in love and leave Albuquerque to start their own lives. Riggs had been there, too. Doing what he did best by watching out for them.

He tossed his shirt onto the bed's headboard to dry. "Didn't do any good, though. Twenty-five years later, and I'm nowhere other than proving Becker's theory was true. Hazel wasn't the only one there that day."

A thought struck her. Fresh and hard. Macie shifted her weight between both feet. "What if Hazel and I weren't the only ones?"

"You mean another victim? Police ran through missing persons reports at the time. I've even gone back to try to establish a pattern, but Hazel's case was unique." Riggs straightened, and suddenly he seemed so much bigger than he had a moment ago. A force to be reckoned with. Not her childhood friend but the detective. More intense, isolated. Focused. "There didn't seem to be any motive, and neither her parents nor her teacher had noticed anything strange going on in her life. They both reported she was her normal wild self. Nothing to suggest the killer targeted her specifically, and there weren't any other open investigations in the area."

"But some killers don't stay in one area, right?" As much as she hated the idea of more victims out there, they needed to consider it now. Macie finally took that full step, bringing herself closer to him as excitement built at the prospect of a new lead to follow. "Sometimes they have to adapt and move to keep from getting caught. I'm not saying whoever did this is a serial offender, but from what I've seen in this town, it's never one incident. Bombers practice their art before the big show. Military units run through their battle plans until they've got it ingrained in their heads. What if Hazel wasn't the first? Or the last?"

She should've thought about it before now. She should've—

"You don't think I've looked? Macie, I'm telling you. There's nothing. No forensics to test. No vehicle to track. No suspects to run background checks on. There's no more crime scene. Everything is gone. Every lead has been exhausted." He almost seemed apologetic and took his own step toward her. Strong hands gripped her arms, holding her upright when the world wanted to crash down around her. "The best chance we have of finding Hazel's killer is finding who murdered my partner."

His redirection hit her harder than she'd expected. That wasn't what they'd agreed on. Macie stepped out of his reach. She'd spent the past two decades trying to get answers. For a moment there, she thought they'd been on the same page, that they'd wanted the same thing, but now...

"I don't understand. You told me you wanted me to stay so we could work together on this. You stopped me from leaving. Twice. What are you saying? You're already giving up?" If she wasn't trying to find Hazel's killer, what was she doing? Who was she? What was she supposed to do with her life? Macie tried to catch her breath, but the temper she'd been warned to keep under control was heating up her chest. "You're just going to forget that she was our best friend and tell me that her case isn't worth continuing? You and Becker have been trying to find her killer all this time, and suddenly you've changed your mind. Why?"

An invisible weight pulled at the sides of his mouth. "Becker and I weren't working Hazel's case together, Macie."

She didn't know what else to say, what to think. Warning triggered in her gut. Telling her to run, to get out of Battle Mountain as fast as possible. Before things got worse.

"A year ago, I put in my papers for a transfer. I got

a new partner," Riggs said. "Becker threw his entire life away for a case that went nowhere. I wasn't going to follow after him."

HE'D NEVER SAID the words before.

Hell, he hadn't even had the guts to say them to Becker.

But the old man had known. He'd tried one last time to get Riggs to come around to his way of thinking before he'd walked off the job, but Riggs hadn't taken the bait. Not again. It'd been too many years wasted in hope, in all-nighters, in empty leads and dead ends. Following Hazel's case had cost him promotions, relationships and time he couldn't ever get back, but Becker hadn't seen any of it. At the end of their partnership, Riggs had finally thrown the truth in his partner's face: he hadn't been building a career of his own. He'd followed Becker's path into the same sad dead end.

And some cases just couldn't be solved.

The storm had come inside while still raging outdoors. He could feel it in Macie's icy gaze, the way she tried to get as far from him in the cramped room as possible by sitting on the bed near the door. Word had come down from BMPD. Roads were closed. Neither of them were going anywhere tonight.

The flowy floral dress that'd brought out the color of her eyes had gone somewhat opaque and dim soaked through, to the point he could tell the color of her matching bra and underwear set, but he didn't have the guts to say anything.

What did you say to someone who'd been caught with several stuffed animals in a sleeping bag in the middle of the woods?

"You can stop staring at me. I'm not going to turn into a monster from the black lagoon." Her hair streaked down her back, and it was then he noted the thin raised line of scarring running from the base of her neck beneath her collar. Had that been from the attack or from something else?

It'd hit him a few minutes before that despite the years they'd known each other, he really didn't know her now. Not as Macie Barclay, at least. What she'd been doing all these years, how she'd survived, if she had a husband or lover or kids. The thought shouldn't have taken so much of his mental energy considering a dead body had brought them together, but he couldn't get the idea of her happy, living a full life while Hazel's had been cut short, out of his head.

"There goes my pitch to the paranormal reality show." He could feel her disappointment like a rock in the pit of his stomach. He knew the feeling all too well. That spark of hope going out. He'd felt it more than a few times over the course of his career.

"Why are you here?" Her words barely registered over the pounding of rain at the window. "You and Becker weren't partners anymore. Why are you the one here trying to solve his murder if you don't want anything to do with the case he was investigating?"

He wasn't sure he could explain it to her. He wasn't sure he could even explain it to himself, but she deserved to know what he'd dragged her into. "Because I'm the reason he's dead."

The words had been there since he'd gotten the hit about a body matching Becker's description turning up in one of the most forgetful towns he'd never found on a map. Right there at the edge of his mind. Nagging, digging, destroying him from the inside out. "The last time I saw him, I told him he'd wasted my life. My career. That he'd stolen twenty-five years I couldn't ever get back. He just looked at me. Didn't even deny it. I think he knew I was right. I think he realized he'd wasted his life, too, and it just pushed him harder. It got him killed."

"Do you really think it's a waste trying to help someone else find peace?" Her question settled between them, and Riggs couldn't help but feel she wasn't asking on Becker's behalf.

"Hazel's already at peace." Didn't anyone get that? Closure wasn't for the victims of the cases he investigated. It was for the living. To give them a sense of justice and finality. "Becker wasn't doing it for her. He was riding that case into the ground for himself. And he was taking me and everyone else in his life down with it."

Macie slid off the bed and took a position at the

window to peer out. "Yet you became a detective because of her. You worked her case until a year ago, believing you could make a difference."

The accusation cut through him. He hadn't told her as much, but he guessed it wasn't hard to put together, either. Or maybe she saw more of him than he'd meant to show. "You're right. I let myself get sucked into the story. I let myself get so focused on trying to find Hazel's killer that I let friendships go, I stopped climbing the department ladder, my family stopped calling. I lost my wife. I was an addict. Just like Becker. I couldn't stop. I couldn't see what the case was costing me. I convinced myself into believing I could be the hero at the end, but it turns out, the entire thing was just a fairy tale. At least until today."

Now it was more like a nightmare.

"You were married?" Macie asked.

"Ten years." Riggs stared at the invisible impression left behind by his wedding band. It wasn't really there. It'd been two years since the divorce, but he could still feel it. That connection to another person. "She saw what was happening and couldn't sit back and watch me do it to myself. I think the divorce was supposed to shock me out of it, but it just made things worse."

"You thought if you could find who killed Hazel, you could get it all back." Macie crossed the room, bringing an air of fresh rain and perfume in her wake. "Maybe your partner did, too. Becker tracked me down. The only reason he'd want to do that is because he believed I had something to add to Hazel's investigation. Whether we like it or not, these two cases are connected. We solve one, we solve the other. Just like you said. Tell me who Becker liked for a suspect."

"No way in hell, Macie. You had the right idea when I found you." Riggs needed to get out of this room. Away from her and childhood memories that had no right to take up space in his head. He should've let her go when he'd had the chance. "Getting involved in a case in which you were a victim isn't going to help Hazel or Becker. You should leave like you intended. Disappear for another twenty-five years."

"I think Becker proved hiding isn't the answer. Look how he found me. Who knows what his killer got out of him before he died. You said it yourself— the best thing we can do is work together. We're stuck inside until the roads are clear. That's not happening until morning." Macie's thin shoulders rose on a deep inhale. "We might as well make the best use of our time."

"That was before I found out you were there when Hazel was abducted." Damn it. He was getting sucked back in. Exactly where he didn't want to be, but she was right. These cases were connected just as he thought, and there was no avoiding the past. No matter how much he wanted to bury it. Riggs dragged his backpack from against the wall and hauled it onto the bed. Tipping the bag upside down, he dumped it empty. "Everything I'm about to show you doesn't leave this room. Understand?"

"These are Becker's belongings? I don't see a laptop or phone." Macie pushed each file and personal item into its separate space across the bed.

"Becker was old school. Didn't trust technology. He used to say murders were solved by detectives. Not computers." The lesson hit Riggs hard when his laptop had crashed with every single note and crime scene photo of one of his first investigations before he'd had a chance to add it to the department server. Although, he wasn't entirely convinced Becker hadn't had something to do with it. Either way, Riggs had gone for physical files after that. Always keeping a backup. "I've already gone through it. He had his keys and his weapon on him. They're with your coroner. I've got a notebook with a couple pages filled in with Becker's handwriting, a pen, a change of clothes, some toiletries. Nothing that points to why he was in that building in the first place or if he was meeting anyone."

Macie flipped through the first few pages of the file, hesitant and tense. Her voice lost some of its confidence. "Seems so…empty."

He reached to take the file from her. "You might not want to look at those."

She dodged his attempt, turning her back to him. "You'd be surprised what I can handle, Detective."

"Riggs." Riggs shoved a hand through his still-damp hair as frustration got the better of him. "Hell, we've known each other for years, woman. You can call me by my first name."

"It's not you," she said. "People I care about end up in danger if I get too close."

Which meant she hadn't built any new relationships all this time. No husband. No lover. No kids. No friends. Macie had isolated herself in the middle of a mountain range to protect the people around her all this time. And, hell, if that wasn't admirable. And heartbreaking. As much as he'd hated the turn his life had taken by following Becker down this never-ending road, he never would've given up their friendship if he'd known their time had been limited. Not for all the promotions in the world.

He wanted to tell Macie she was safe. That she could trust him, and that nothing bad was going to happen to her, but it'd be a lie. Becker had died with Macie's contact information in his pocket. It stood to reason whoever'd killed Hazel—whoever'd abducted them as kids—knew she was here.

And hunting her.

Riggs took a step forward, still aware of her personal space. "I know you're scared, but I'm not going to let anything happen to you, Macie. I give you my word."

"I made that same promise to Hazel once. That I'd always protect her and have her back. She said the same thing to me. We made a blood oath because we thought we could make it last forever." Macie flipped her right palm upward as a glimmer of tears welled in her eyes. "Look how that turned out."

He dared another step and reached out. Only this time, it wasn't for the case file. Running his thumb down the middle of her palm, he memorized the raised tissue there. So many scars. "I think you're forgetting I'm not a ten-year-old girl."

Her laugh scattered the pressure building in his chest. "No. You're definitely not. You're a lot more hairy, for one thing."

"Is that a bad thing?" He stroked his five-o'clock shadow, and suddenly felt himself wanting to shave it all off. For her. Which was crazy. He hadn't shaved for anyone, and he didn't intend to start now.

"Not when it's in all the right places." Macie's smile held on longer than he'd expected, but she pulled her hand away. Her focus diverted to the file in her other hand. "This isn't the official case file."

"What do you mean?" Riggs maneuvered over her shoulder to get a better look, getting a lungful of damp hair and soft perfume.

"I've seen the original investigation file for Hazel's case. I know exactly what's inside. This isn't it." She folded the manila file cover to the back, exposing the first page of witness interview statements from twenty-five years ago. "None of these names are familiar."

To him, either. Riggs pried the file from her hand and checked the tab on the side. Something fell from inside and hit the floor. "This doesn't make sense. Becker was extreme when it came to keeping his files clean. Why would there be another file in here?"

"Because Becker wasn't just investigating Hazel's case." Macie collected the photo that'd dropped and handed it off. A crime scene photo, foreign and un-recognizable. "He'd found another victim."

Chapter Five

Sakari Vigil.

Seven years old.

She'd gone missing from her backyard in Dulce, New Mexico, in the blink of an eye. Ten years ago.

One minute she'd been playing in the hose, running through the grass when her mother had gone in to get some more sunscreen and water. The next Sakari had been gone. Three days later, her body had been laid peacefully on the eastern border of the Jicarilla Apache reservation.

Macie's heart hurt as she traced the smile creases around the girl's eyes in the photo. Another victim. The blow had taken the fight right out of her. According to Becker's notes, Dulce police had exhausted every lead within a month. No suspects. No leads within the past few years. The case had gone as cold as Hazel's. "Becker never said anything to you about another victim? About how he'd come to find her?"

"No." Riggs stared out the single window at the

back of the room, unmoving and braced against the wall. Quiet. She couldn't read him as well as she used to, but she could feel the same tendril of pain in him. The one that wound tighter with every breath. "Nothing."

"There's a pattern here." Macie hated that fact. That this killer wasn't choosing his victims randomly but looking for a carefully thought-out set of parameters. How many other victims had fallen into the sickening set of rules he'd set? How many more were out there they weren't seeing? "Hazel and Sakari were both only children. He wanted to make sure he could get them alone—that other siblings wouldn't interfere or be able to identify him."

Riggs slid his hand down the cringeworthy wallpaper. "Then why attack Hazel when she was with you?"

She had an answer, but Macie didn't have the guts to tell him the truth. Not yet. "He might not have planned for me to be there that day."

"There's fifteen years between these cases. We can't even be sure both girls were killed by the same person." Riggs shoved away from the wall. "For all we know, Becker was grasping at straws, chasing after another one of his dead ends."

She didn't think so. "Both victims were strangled. The pattern left behind on their throats is similar. Same gender. Same family dynamic. Taken from outdoors. Close in age."

But that raised the question: Why hadn't the Criminal Justice Information System linked the two cases?

"No. They're not." Riggs ripped the photo of Sakari from her hand and turned it to face her, and in that moment, she saw the truth. The agony in his expression. The debilitating guilt contorting his handsome face into something other and dangerous. "Sakari Vigil was seven years old, Macie. Seven. She was waiting for her mom to bring her some water when she got too hot from playing in the backyard. Not climbing up a mountain without telling anyone where she was going. She was innocent."

Her defenses dumped a dose of adrenaline into her veins. "I'm going to pretend you didn't just blame me or Hazel for what happened that day she went missing, Detective."

"That's not… That's not what I meant." He shook his head as though he could rewind time and try again. "I'm sorry. I just—"

"You want a reason. A motive." Because if they could make one element of this case make sense, the rest would follow. That was how it was supposed to work. But Macie had been at this long enough to know one puzzle piece did not a painting of Lake Como make. "You want someone to blame."

"Yes." That single word pained her more than any other they'd said in the past hour. Riggs practically stumbled back, that photo still in his hand. "Now instead of solving Becker's murder, there are two families out there wondering what happened to their little girls. Who knows how many others?"

The intense detective who hadn't taken no for an answer this morning retreated into the man who'd put so many others ahead of him. Always searching for answers with no hope of achieving a molecule of something significant. The one who'd lost and given up having anyone important in his life for one more chance to do something good. Riggs Karig wasn't like the officers she'd worked with these past few years. Sure, they'd all had their reasons for joining Battle Mountain PD. A job, a trauma or a sense of duty, but Riggs… He took every case personally. It was that kind of commitment that would consume him in the end. "Have you considered homicide investigations might not be the right career choice for you?"

The question seemed to knock him out of whatever downward cycle he was circling. "I was working Becker's path. Not mine."

"But you could've stopped." Macie didn't miss the fact she could have, too. That she could've thrown away the files and photos and reports she'd pinned to the inside of her closet and forgotten about Hazel. That she could've let someone in these past few years, just to take the weight off her shoulders and feel what it was like to trust another person again.

That she could've fallen in love or traveled the world or learned to bake all those delicious treats like Reagan. She could've had a whole life had she not chosen to live in the past. "You could've altered your course. Unless there was something you were hoping to find along the way. Something that would've made all this worth it."

Riggs collapsed back against the wall, staring down at the same photo of Sakari Vigil as she had. "There was something. I used to have this friend. She changed my life. Not in any big way, but she made an effort with me. I couldn't say that about anyone else really. Not my parents. Not my brother or my teachers. To them, I was and always would be a screwup. I couldn't do anything right, but to this friend, she treated me like a person. She shared her lunches with me because all I had was a pudding cup that day. She helped me with my homework when math wasn't making sense, and I was on the verge of repeating fifth grade. She made me laugh all the time, except for when she punched me in the nose because I'd pulled her hair."

Macie's insides clenched at the memory. He wasn't just talking about a friend he'd had over the years. He was talking about her.

"One day, she was just gone, and I was back to being alone." That ache she'd felt solidified in his voice. "I thought maybe if I solved Hazel's case, she'd come back. That we'd pick up right where we left off. Until I realized my entire life had passed me by, and I'd fallen for another fantasy."

Her throat threatened to close in and she collapsed back onto the edge of the bed. Macie tried to swallow around it, but the words weren't there. "I... I had no idea."

"Would it have changed anything if you did?" Sincerity laced every word. They both knew the answer. Her parents had dragged her from Albuquerque in fear for her life. Nothing and no one would've been able to convince them otherwise.

"No," she said.

Riggs closed the distance between them, before setting the photo of Sakari Vigil back onto the file in her lap. "Becker broke protocol. Each case is supposed to have its own separate file, but he combined these two. He was working them as the same case."

"There's another possibility." Macie straightened the file's contents with the side of her finger. "People who hurt others—like the ones I've seen—all have one thing in common. They don't want to get caught. Serial killers, bombers, gunmen—they're all the same. They'll do whatever it takes to keep their freedom, including following media coverage, learning who's involved in the investigation and even taking official pieces out of the game. It's possible Becker knew he was being lured to that building and was compelled to hand over whatever he had. He could've shoved both files in here while handing over an empty folder or one stuffed with random paperwork. The killer most likely knew he liked to keep physical notes. By moving both files to the same folder, Becker could've been protecting the investigation by giving up a decoy."

Riggs stared at her a moment, seemingly in a daze. "You're starting to sound like a detective."

"I might've picked up a few things over the years." Pride and a hint of confidence speared through her. As much as she'd hidden herself from the chief and his officers, none of them had bothered to try to get to know her. She was Macie the Dispatcher—a tool to make their jobs easier. Someone with connections and a tree house to hide out in or a babysitter when they needed to respond to a call. Would any of them have guessed she might know more about Battle Mountain and the people in it than they did? "Hard not to in a town like this."

Riggs moved away from the wall, a little more stable on his feet from the look of it. The storm that'd taken him at his most vulnerable had passed, leaving behind an air of capability and experience. Most of the men who'd tried to insert themselves into her life had kept their masculine armor in place. No emotion. No hint of weakness. It was kind of nice to see one of them break, even just for a couple minutes.

"Dulce is about three hours north of Albuquerque along the freeway."

Macie pulled a map up on her phone, and her stomach flipped. He was right. If they were looking for the same killer in both cases, following the freeway from Albuquerque north took him straight through Dulce, and if he kept going north… "Battle Mountain is on that route."

"Where Becker was killed," Riggs said.

Macie didn't want to think about the implications. She didn't want to think of another little girl like Sakari and Hazel being ripped from her family and found three days later. Penny's face materialized at the back of her mind. No. She couldn't think like that. Penny was just four years old. Way too young to be drawn into a case like this, and someone stupid enough to even come near her would suffer the wrath of the entire Battle Mountain police department.

"Let's say Becker was right. Sakari Vigil was killed by the same unsub as Hazel. Whoever we're dealing with, it's not compulsion." Riggs cut another path through the limited space between the foot of the bed and the dresser. So close. "Becker's death was an outlier, a means to an end, but Sakari and Hazel… They're the real data. He's able to hold himself off for years at a time. He's in control, able to make smart decisions. Not being overcome by his needs. If that's the case, why kill Becker after all these years? Why not take him off the board long before now?"

"Could be whoever is doing this was incarcerated. The killer might've been forced to take a break, but without a name to run, that doesn't get us anywhere." There was another reason she could think of. "Maybe it was like you said, you'd never gotten close. No suspects. No new leads or witnesses. Becker must've surprised him. He must've followed the killer here, to Battle Mountain."

Tingling spread down her arms and into her fingers locked around the file. It was only then she realized the rain had stopped. The roads would open soon, and there'd be no reason for her to stay. No reason to keep following this path. Macie studied that smiling face a second time.

Every cell in her body homed in on Riggs. There was no turning back. No running this time. His partner had come to Battle Mountain for a reason, maybe even to stop another little girl from being taken. "He's on the hunt for a new victim."

HE SHOULD'VE KNOWN whoever'd killed Hazel wasn't finished.

He'd just been too stubborn to see what Becker had seen.

Riggs rolled over on the bed. Paper crumpled beneath him. Then he felt nothing but a wall of warmth.

Forcing his eyes open, he realized he was face-to-face with Macie. She was still asleep, curled on her side with her mouth slightly parted. Long lashes fanned out across the tops of her cheeks. This close, each lash distinct. Not clumped together with mascara or anything else to hide her natural beauty. A spatter of freckles stood out across her nose that he hadn't noticed until now, and Riggs found himself counting them to block out the world a little longer.

"You're staring again." Her voice cracked on the last word, attesting to how late they'd gone through Becker's file last night. Over and over. No notes as to who his partner had suspected killed the two victims, but he had to have some idea. Why else come to Battle Mountain? Why go to that building?

"Sorry. I had to pinch myself to see if I was dreaming," he said. "Can't remember the last time I woke up to a woman in my bed. At least one that wasn't permanently pissed at me."

Macie pressed herself upright, a yawn peeling back that guarded, sarcastic layer. Look at that. She was real. "Keep pushing your luck. I'm sure you'll get there."

She'd finally given in to changing out of her dress, going for what looked like an oversize men's T-shirt and sweats from her duffel bag. Part of him had wondered whose shirt she'd taken over while the other part lectured him how it was none of his business.

They weren't together. Hell, they weren't even real partners.

They'd been brought together by a dead man.

Riggs peeled the scattered papers of their handwritten notes from beneath his rib cage. "I'd offer you some breakfast, but apparently this isn't one of those fancy places, and I'm pretty sure the owner hates me."

"Cindy? No. She hates everybody." Her laugh tendrilled through his chest and set up residence in his stomach. "Besides, why settle for motel breakfast when Greta's is just up the street."

"Does everyone in this town name their establishments after themselves?" he asked.

Macie scooted off the end of the bed with more grace than he had on a shooting range. Frizz haloed around the crown of her head. Every hair out of place. Quite a change from the hell-raiser he'd met at her front door yesterday. "If they have any chance of surviving around here, yeah. I'm going to get dressed. I won't be long."

"Take your time." He braced himself against her pillow, aggravating a hint of her perfume. The bathroom door clicked closed, and Riggs took the chance to breathe in her light scent. It was calming and invigorating at the same time. Familiar but fresh. It was all Macie, and he'd be lying to himself if he said he didn't like it.

He checked his phone. Two missed calls. One from

his captain, the other from a number he didn't recognize. Dragging himself to the edge of the bed, Riggs popped his neck and shook off the near hangover from lack of sleep and too much talking into the early morning hours. He hit the unfamiliar number and waited.

"Oh, good. Macie hasn't killed you and disposed of your body yet." Easton Ford's voice came with a sudden need to salute and stand up straight. The interim chief had obviously been up for hours, even though the old clock radio on the nightstand read seven in the morning. Military man, through and through. "One less thing on my plate I have to worry about."

"That happen often?" Riggs glanced toward the bathroom door. "Her disposing of bodies?"

"Only to the people she doesn't like," Ford said. "Which is a lot of people, mind you, including me."

"Can't imagine how you've managed to stay alive all this time." Joking aside, he and Easton Ford weren't friends. They were trying to solve the Becker murder and stop a killer from striking again, but humor had long been used as a way to diffuse the tension and violence police faced on a daily basis. It was the only way to survive. "You got something for me?"

"Our coroner is doing the autopsy on your guy today. Thought you might want to be part of the action," Ford said.

"Sounds like a party." He and Macie had gone through everything Becker had kept in his combined file. It made sense his partner had wanted to protect the investigation, but now they had the problem of sorting through notes that could pertain to either case. Only Becker would've been able to tell the difference. Riggs stole another glance at the thin door separating him from the woman on the other side. "Let me ask you something. You ever hear anything about Macie being found in the middle of the woods in a sleeping bag with a bunch of stuffed animals?"

Well, hell, that was a sentence he hadn't ever thought he'd hear himself say. His brain had worked through the night, conjuring different scenarios. Some of them outside the natural law of man. Or woman.

"Please tell me she didn't order a blonde coffee from Caffeine and Carbs." Ford sounded as though he was having a hard time keeping his laugh to himself, and Riggs's curiosity rocketed into overdrive.

What the hell had he gotten himself into here? "I think she tossed it before she got the full effect."

"Let's just say you dodged a bullet. Macie and caffeine don't mix well." Shuffling cut through from the other end of the line. "Penny, not the phone!"

The other side of the line cut short.

Checking the screen, he confirmed the call had ended. Seemed Easton Ford had his hands just as full as Riggs. He made quick work of collecting their notes from last night and organizing everything back into the file as best he could. He changed his clothes faster than he ever had before.

But not fast enough.

The bathroom door swung open. Macie froze, her eyes wide, and he couldn't even blame the smile hitching higher on her mouth. His foot had gotten caught in his pant leg. He'd spent the past few seconds hopping, trying to get it free without falling over. Solely in his boxers. Damn it.

She leaned against the doorframe, crossing her arms. All that fiery hair had been tamed as though she'd come straight out of a salon. Absolutely beautiful in another one of her flowy dresses. This one a deep green with peach flowers that brought out the brightness in her cheeks.

Riggs collapsed against the bed. He finally got his foot free. "Ever heard of a little thing called privacy?"

"Privacy is what you get in a bathroom with a closed door. Not in the middle of the motel room. Besides, I'm not sure why you're being so shy. Compared to most of the guys around here, you, Detective, are a masterpiece. I wouldn't mind adding you to my private collection." Disbelief brought her out of pure amusement into full-on excitement as she closed the distance between them. Wrapping one hand around his arm, Macie forced him to his feet and turned his backside to face her. "Wait. Is that a unicorn, a rainbow and a cat on your ass?"

Unfiltered heat penetrated through his arm and up his neck at her touch. It shot into his gut and exploded into something cleansing and addictive. The reaction triggered him to pull away and get back some control. Riggs ripped his dry T-shirt from off the back of the headboard and shoved his head through the collar. "For your information, I forgot to pack a change of clothes. These were the only pair I could find at the gas station on my way into town."

He managed to get his arms through the correct holes.

"Well, to be fair, I think there's a unicorn inside all of us." That smile was back—the one that couldn't even compare to the way her touch had affected him on a cellular level. "Not sure about cats, though."

"The only thing inside of me is an empty stomach, the urge to solve this case and get back to my life." Riggs shoved his feet into his boots and laced them into place, but his brain just couldn't help sticking on the fact she'd said she wanted to add him to her private collection. Who said exactly what they were thinking like that?

"If I only had a nickel for all the times I've heard those exact words." Macie dragged a small purse from her duffel bag and set it over her shoulder.

"Come on, Detective. Let's get you something to eat before that unicorn turns into a bear."

"If I turn into a bear, does that mean I'll end up in your sleeping bag in the middle of the woods after too much coffee?" Riggs couldn't help himself.

"If you're not careful, you'll end up down one of the mineshafts where no one will find your body." Her tone lacked any humor, and a sliver of fear prickled down the back of his neck.

Still, this game they'd created had him wanting more. It reminded him of the stupid jokes and threats they'd thrown at each other growing up in New Mexico. This side of her he knew, and hell, if he was being honest, it was a side that he'd missed.

His phone rang from his back pocket. Same number he'd called back a few minutes ago. Riggs answered, one finger held up at Macie's questioning expression. "Don't tell me the autopsy already started, Ford. It's been two minutes."

"Bring Macie back to the station. Now." The older Ford brother couldn't catch his breath from what it sounded like, and a wave of battle-ready tension flooded through Riggs.

His gaze met Macie's. In an instant, their bizarre humor was shoved aside as he gauged her reaction and what to do next. "Something happened."

"She's gone." Clattering—something like a chair hitting a wall or the floor—filtered through Easton

Ford's heavy breathing. "I can't find her anywhere. The gun is here, but she isn't. She knows not to leave the station while she's here. She knows to check in every few minutes."

Riggs didn't understand. "Slow down, Ford. Who? Who's gone?"

"Penny." Both sides of the phone met with silence for a series of seconds. "She's been taken."

Chapter Six

"I trusted you!" Campbell Dwyer shoved the interim chief against the wall, her hands fisted in his uniform. And Easton Ford let it happen. "You promised me she was safe here, Easton. How did this happen? How could you not check to make sure the doors were locked!"

Macie joined Campbell's husband—Kendric Hudson—in trying to pry Campbell off the chief. A lot of good she could do up against a fully trained investigator more comfortable with a loaded gun in her hand than Penny's favorite toy. Campbell was former Colorado Bureau of Investigation. She worked Internal Affairs while mothering a sociopathic four-year-old and standing up to the man who'd left her as a single parent after an explosion had destroyed his world and half his face. Tears streaked down Campbell's face as she ripped free of Macie's hands and pushed at her husband. Kendric obviously knew better than to try anything else. The woman was a force to be reckoned with outside CBI as much as she had been inside.

"I did, Campbell. I swear it. The back door was locked when I checked in with her twenty minutes ago." Easton straightened, ready to take another attack like the good soldier he was supposed to be. "You know I would never fail to secure this place."

"So what then?" Campbell asked. "Someone just walked through the front door and grabbed her?"

"The back door is unlocked now." Easton's voice turned to glass. "There aren't any fresh scratches on the dead bolt plate, which means they knew what they were doing."

Macie reached out to Campbell, but instantly knocked back into a wall of muscle she'd forgotten had followed her inside. Riggs. He kept her upright, as though ready to shove her back into the ring. "Campbell, we're going to find her. Okay? I know what you must be feeling, but she can't have gotten far."

The grieving mother turned all that rage and uncertainty on Macie. "No. You don't. You don't know, Macie. You're a dispatcher. You're not a cop, and you're not a mother. You have no idea what really goes on outside of this station, and you were supposed to be here. You were supposed to watch her. Where the hell were you?"

Shock slapped her across the face as efficiently as a physical strike. "I…" She wanted to lean into

Riggs's strength. She wanted to explain that she hadn't left Penny alone, but that she was trying to find a killer. None of the words would take shape, and a sickening wrenching twisted her insides.

"Campbell, this isn't her fault." Kendric eased his hand around his wife's arm. "Gregson and Majors are out searching Main Street now. Isla and Adan are combing through the neighborhoods, and Karie Ford is keeping an eye out at the ranch. The entire department is on our side. We will find her."

"No. I will find her. Because this wasn't supposed to happen again. Because I promised her this wasn't going to happen again." Something heavy and suffocating drained from Campbell's face, leaving a shadow of the woman Macie knew. It was the same look she'd noted on Hazel's mother's face when the police had finally found the body. Campbell turned into Kendric's chest, but she didn't stop for comfort. She pointed a strong finger into Easton's face—one of the few daring enough to confront the older Ford. That, in and of itself, was enough for Macie to like her, but hurt set up residence where admiration had flourished. Penny had been kidnapped once before. Taken by a madman determined to get away with murder and left for dead in a shed in the middle of winter woods. Campbell and Kendric had fought like hell to get her back, and Campbell was right. Macie had no idea what it felt like to lose something so precious. "You and I both know this never would've happened if Weston was still in charge. You and I aren't finished."

Easton didn't answer, didn't even seem to breathe as Kendric followed Campbell toward the front of the station and out onto the street. Macie had no doubt in her mind Campbell would do whatever it took to find their daughter. But this killer... The one who'd taken Hazel and Sakari... He didn't play by the same rules BMPD followed.

A tremor worked up Macie's arms. Penny was gone. Someone had come into a police station and taken her right under the nose of the most volatile officer in command, and it was her fault. "We have three days to find her."

"You can't know that." Easton had started showing signs of life, but that legendary guard was back in place.

"Actually, we do." Riggs took position at her side. He handed over the case file they'd analyzed more times than Macie could count last night. "As I said yesterday, Becker was working on a twenty-five-year-old case. It's what brought him to Battle Mountain. Hazel McAdams. We believe he was following a suspect from Albuquerque and found who he was looking for here. Killer must've recognized him. Strangled him before my partner could do anything about it. Both victims Becker identified were missing for three days. It's a pattern. One we're still trying to work out."

"You said both victims." Easton started reading the file. "Hazel McAdams. Found strangled next to a creek in the woods. What makes you think Penny's disappearance is the work of the same attacker?"

"We discovered another case combined with the McAdams case last night, taken from Becker's car." Macie's mouth dried. She didn't even want to think about the sweet girl she'd gotten to know the past couple months found with bruises around her neck. Penny was feisty. She was stubborn, but she wouldn't be able to overcome a full-grown man alone. The only way Macie had been able to escape was with help. And Hazel had died because of it. That urge to lean into Riggs again, to borrow some of his strength, took hold, and Macie let her arm settle against his. His gaze dipped to the point where their skin touched, but he didn't pull away. "A seven-year-old girl strangled outside the reservation in Dulce ten years ago. Missing three days, just like Hazel."

"These notes refer to Avalynn Davis, Hazel's best friend at the time she went missing." Easton Ford set that unreadable gaze on her. "You knew the first victim. That's why Detective Becker came to find you, right?"

He couldn't possibly know that. "How...how do you..."

"I like to know everything I can about the people coming near this department and my family, just in case," Easton said. "When I learned the name Macie

Barclay didn't surface until around nineteen years ago, I took a deeper look at you."

"You never said anything." The words barely registered over the kick of the air conditioner. She'd lied to the chief, to Easton, to everyone out of survival, but the sudden possibility of being punished for it—of losing all this—hurt more than she'd expected. "You just gave me dagger eyes every time we were in the same room together."

"People change their names for a lot of reasons. I figured you'd tell us yours when you were ready." Easton handed off the file to her.

"Us." Oh, no. Macie was practically using Riggs to balance now. "So Weston knows, too."

"Weston knows, but he's not keen on sharing that information with the rest of the department. Like I said, I protect my family, Macie. That includes you when the mood strikes." Easton turned on Riggs, leaving her exhausted and shocked and on edge at the same time. "Your name is in that file, too, Detective. Funny how you failed to mention that part when you met with me after Kevin Becker's body was found. Riggs Karig, also best friends with the first victim."

"Yes, sir." Riggs cut his attention to her and held her there for what seemed like a minute straight. "Hazel, Macie and I grew up together. We were the first to be interviewed during the investigation."

He called her Macie. It shouldn't have held so much significance, but it did. Like he was accepting the woman she'd become. That she wasn't the girl he'd known anymore.

But Macie had worked in this department long enough to know what Easton would say next. That they were too close to the case. That personal feelings didn't have any right to be involved in an investigation. That connections to the victim would only lead to mistakes. He was going to forbid them to help with the search or dig deeper into Becker's notes. They'd end up on the bench or worse. Riggs would be sent back to Albuquerque to resume his life, and she'd…keep running.

She studied Riggs out of the corner of her eye. Twenty-four hours. That was all it'd taken for him to get back beneath her skin. All she'd wanted to do was get away from him this time yesterday. Now it felt as though he fit. Here in Battle Mountain.

"Then you two are the ones who have the most to lose if you don't get out there and find Penny." Easton turned back into the office that wasn't his. Only this time, Macie didn't get nausea thinking about him behind that desk. He paused in the doorframe, one hand overlapping the butt on his gun. "Just promise me one thing, Macie. Promise you're not going to try to curse me again. I can't take the acid reflux." Ford closed the door, effectively ending their conversation.

She didn't know where revealing her real identity left them or this department, but Macie was sure of one thing: there was a scared little girl out there because of her.

Riggs maneuvered between her and the chief's door, consuming her attention until the world dissolved around them. "I know what you're thinking, Macie. I don't care what Penny's mom said. This isn't your fault. You couldn't have possibly known—"

"If I hadn't run, he never would've followed me here. He never would've killed Sakari or targeted Penny in the first place. You and I both know this isn't about them. It's about me. The one who got away." The weight of the knowledge was comforting in a way. They had a motive now. "He'll take her somewhere isolated. Like the woods. Somewhere no one will hear her scream for help. Both victims were found with small amounts of water in their lungs, so I think he'll want to hole up near the lake or a creek. He might even use it to control her."

Riggs nodded agreement. He believed her, like she knew what she was talking about. She couldn't remember a time when anyone else had taken her word for anything. It was just as Campbell had said. She wasn't a cop. When it came right down to police matters, what did she know? "You got a place in mind?"

"Yeah." Macie steeled herself in confidence. "I do."

THE TREES WERE closing in.

Too many shadows. Too much movement. Too much for his senses to process. Damp earth, rustling leaves, the humidity clinging to his skin—all of it worked to break his concentration.

Riggs followed in Macie's footsteps along only one of the rivers weaving out of the south end of Lake San Cristobal. They'd already covered one of the creeks that'd dead-ended and were now making their way north to catch the source of the second. He batted away at something that zinged straight into his face right before something salty and bitter spread across his tongue. "I think I just ate a bug."

"It won't be the last one. After a while, you get used to it. They become protein rather than a nuisance," she said.

He wasn't sure he ever wanted to view insects as a food source, but Riggs was out of his element here. If it came right down to survival, he bet there wasn't much of anything he wouldn't try. Especially if someone he cared about was in danger.

Macie charged ahead, all determination and defiance. That stubborn drive he'd tried to avoid as a kid had ramped up full force in the face of finding a four-year-old girl. She blamed herself. For not being at the station when Penny had been taken, for not being able to comfort the girl's mother, for the fact Penny had gone missing in the first place. He could see it in the way she refused to slow down despite the mosquito bites at the back of her neck and how she clung to the water gun she'd found under one of the chairs at the station. Nothing he said would change her mind or make her see any different.

Then again, maybe that stubbornness was what was going to bring Penny home.

They hadn't found any traces of activity yet. No footprints. Not even a granola bar wrapper or signs of an ATV. It was looking like whoever'd taken Penny hadn't come this way. His muscles ached. He'd sweat as much as he'd had to drink in the past hour, and he was out of breath. How Macie managed to keep going after nearly two hours of searching, he had no idea. "I don't know how you do it. As much as I hate to admit this, I've gotta take a break."

"Okay." She veered toward one of the trees off to her right, its roots clawing up through the ground like fingers waiting to take her into the dark. Stripping free from the jacket she'd changed into, Macie took a seat at the base and chugged a mouthful of water from her bottle. "We're about a mile from the source of the next river. Should make it there by sunset if we keep up this pace. We'll need the flashlights we brought."

Riggs swiped his mouth with the back of his hand. "My teeth feel like the grille on my SUV."

"Look like it too from here." She set her head back against the bark and closed her eyes. Sweat glistened on her skin, but Macie wasn't the kind of woman to admit she'd lost her fight more than two miles ago.

She dumped a good portion of water over her head. "I won't hold it against you."

"We're going to need entire teams of people and K9s to cover this area, Macie. We can't keep going like this all night." They'd come into this area on a hunch, a mere connection between both victims, but what if they were wrong? What if Penny wasn't here like Macie believed? What if they were wasting what precious time the girl had left looking in the wrong place? "For all we know, she's not even out here."

"She is. I can feel it." She pushed herself to her feet. "I'm not giving up."

But feelings didn't solve cases. Evidence did, and so far, they hadn't found any. Time was running out for Penny, and he sure as hell didn't want to be the one to have to tell Macie she was wrong. Riggs straightened. "I'm not telling you to give up. I'm asking you to be realistic."

"You want me to be realistic?" Exhaustion etched into her expression. Her hair was out of place again, her skin sallower around her cheekbones. In a matter of hours, she'd gone from a woman on the run to a woman who had something to stay for, but it'd come at a cost. "Here's reality, Riggs. Penny is scared. She's alone, possibly hurt, and she's already been through this once before. Someone took her from her family to punish them, and now it's happening all over again. An entire department of police officers weren't able to keep her safe. Only this time, he's punishing me. So you can go back to the car or rest as long as you need. You can go back to Albuquerque and your life and keep pretending Hazel's case doesn't affect you anymore, but I'm not leaving until I find that girl."

His heart gripped hard in his chest. Riggs tugged a flashlight from his backpack and compressed the power button. Night would fall fast. There was no way in hell he was going to leave her out here to face it alone. "Okay. One hour."

Macie notched her chin higher, daring him to ask a single thing of her. "What?"

"Going like this half-cocked, desperate, alone and in the dark isn't helping Penny. So I want your word. We turn back in an hour." Riggs hiked the short distance between them. "If we haven't found anything by then, we regroup at the station and come up with another plan. We get ourselves a search team to hit the ground in the morning. We call in whoever the hell we need to call in and start fresh. Give her a real chance of being found."

"One hour?" An internal war played across her face. Push herself to find something—anything—out here that could give them an idea of where Penny was, or do the logical thing and come back to search a much larger area with help. Macie checked her smartwatch. Large numbers ticked down in the limited light still penetrating through the trees. "Fine."

"After you." Riggs set his attention to the ground,

keeping Macie's boots in his peripheral vision as he scoured the dirt and plant life for signs of disturbance. The forest fire that'd eaten through a good chunk of the woods hadn't come this far south, but he could still smell the char in the air. Insects trilled within bark and under bushes, out of sight, and set his nerves on high alert. Too many places to hide in here. Not enough knowledge of the area. All he had was Macie. "I'm sorry. About Penny. From the way you two were drenching each other with those water guns, seems like you were—are—close."

Riggs wanted to kick himself for the slip. Penny wasn't dead. Not yet. He had to believe the killer would stick to his MO. That he would give them three days to catch up and bring her home.

"I'm not sure it's possible to be close to a four-year-old." Macie didn't lose a step as she answered, hauling herself over a fallen tree. They were still following the creek they'd already searched, but the water was traveling faster now. They were getting closer to the source threading out of the lake. "All they care about is when they're getting a snack and if you're going to make them take a nap."

His laugh caught him off guard. A branch scraped along the sleeve of his jacket, and he noted the trees had grown thicker in this section of the woods. "Still, she obviously trusts you. I don't know about you, but I don't let just anyone shoot me with freezing cold water."

"She likes to give people hugs when she's soaked. It's their surprise, I think. Their screams make her laugh." Macie's voice dipped an octave. "The first time she did it to Easton, I nearly fell off my chair. You should've seen his face…" She stopped dead in her tracks, every muscle in her body wound tight.

The humor they'd shared had died in a matter of seconds. Riggs set his hand on her shoulder, but she didn't move. "We're going to find her, Mace. We're not giving up."

"Riggs, is that…" She pointed to a clump of fur caught on one of the lower branches.

He stepped around her, before tearing it free. No. Not fur. Hair. Blond with slight waves. Just like Penny's. Son of a bitch. Macie had been right. Riggs scanned the immediate area. Arm stretched out, he maneuvered Macie back from the spot. No footprints. No ATV treads. Nothing to support they were on the right track. "She was here."

A rough exhale escaped Macie's control. "Penny! Penny, can you hear me! It's Macie. I'm here!"

They listened for a series of seconds. No answer. But if their theory was right—that Penny had been taken from the station—had they really expected one?

The same awareness of being watched that he'd experienced back at Macie's tree house dug through him. "Macie, quiet."

"Penny!" She stepped off the trail they'd followed and closer to the trees.

Movement registered from the tree line to his right.

He shoved Macie to the ground, but not fast enough. Pain ignited along his arm as they landed in a tangle of limbs and gasps. He clamped a hand over the wound, but the knife had embedded deep into his shoulder.

"Riggs!" She pulled her legs out from under him, her hands hovering above the wound.

"Macie, go." He hauled himself to his feet. He unholstered his gun and took aim into the darkness. Only he couldn't see a damn thing. His vision wavered, and Riggs stumbled to his left. A growl clawed up his throat, and he dropped to his knees. He tried to get to his feet, but he was losing too much blood. "I'll cover you. Run."

"I'm not leaving you." She tried to hold him steady. Coming around to his front, she shoved him along the trail. "Come on. We can make it."

"No." An outline separated from the trees. "You can't."

Riggs raised his weapon to take aim, but the world went black.

Chapter Seven

A soft vibration reverberated through her wrist.

Music filled her head, but she wasn't sure where it was coming from. Macie tried to open her eyes. All she met was darkness. Cold, cold darkness. Her throat burned from dropping temperatures, like she'd been left exposed to elements. A shiver prickled at her arms. "Riggs?"

Something snapped to her left.

Shoving to sit upright, she leveraged her heels into the ground. The crunch of leaves filled her ears. She was outside. Still in the woods? "Hello?"

Silence pressed in around her. Slices of memory—of blood, of pain, of desertion—filled the gaps. Penny. They'd found a lock of her hair. And Riggs... Her entire body shuddered as she struggled to her feet. He'd been stabbed. So much blood. She could feel it dried in her palms. Someone had attacked them. "Penny?"

"She's not going to answer, Avalynn," an unfamiliar voice said. "In fact, she won't be saying anything at all for a while."

Fear tripled the nausea churning in her stomach, and Macie collapsed into the tree at her back. She searched her immediate surroundings. She couldn't see him, didn't know where his voice had come from. But he could see her. She was sure of it. Her fingertips clawed into the bark as though she could use it as a weapon. She hadn't been strong enough to fight back then, but she could do this for Penny. She could bring her home. "It's you, isn't it?"

"I've been looking for you for twenty-five years," he said. "Canada, New York, California, Montana. I lost you in Colorado. Turns out, all this time you've been in my own backyard."

All the places she'd hidden, never staying put for too long. Because she'd felt like she was being followed. And if what he said was true, she'd been right. Until she'd come to Battle Mountain. This place had provided safety and protection when no other could. Now she knew why. The same terror she'd felt at the edge of that creek when strong arms had locked around her took hold. Macie tried to control the wobble of her bottom lip. She had to focus. "Where is Penny?"

The voice came from her right this time. "Don't worry. I've taken such good care of her."

"She doesn't have anything to do with this." Macie braced herself to leave the protection of the tree.

Bending at the knees, she skimmed the ground for something—anything—she could use as a weapon in case her attacker came closer. "She's just a little girl. You have me. You can let her go home to her family."

"But you and I both know the truth about little girls, don't we, Avalynn?" He'd moved again, circling behind her. This was all a game to him. Predator versus prey, but she wasn't going to play. Not fairly, anyway. "They're so much stronger than they look. As long as Penny does exactly as I say, she'll be fine."

"You mean until you get bored of her." Her fingers brushed thin sticks and soggy leaves. Cold settled in the tips of her fingers and toes. She needed something heavy, something that could inflict damage if she had any chance of finding Penny. "The same way you got bored of Hazel and killed her."

"Hazel should've done as I asked." Anger intensified the bite in his words, and dread pooled at the base of Macie's spine. "She knew exactly what she was doing when she tried to escape, and she paid the price for that choice. Just as you'll pay for yours."

The strike came out of nowhere.

It crashed into the side of her face and knocked her off-balance. Macie hit the ground as lightning struck behind her eyes. Rolling onto her side, she tried to crawl back to the tree she'd abandoned, but a second punch took vital air straight from her lungs.

"Do you remember that day I found you in the

woods, Avalynn?" The voice was quieter now. Distant and low. Like he'd crouched to watch her struggle. "Do you remember what you did to me?"

Her face pulsed in rhythm to her heartbeat. Macie tried to get onto all fours, but the pain was too much. "Where are they? Where are Penny and Riggs?"

"You elbowed me in the face. Broke my cheekbone if you can believe it." Shuffling filled the night. Purposeful. Trying to pull her focus. "The bone never set right. Now it always looks like I'm smiling. I've replayed that moment in my head so many times."

Stinging pain rippled across her scalp as a strong hand fisted her hair. Her attacker dragged her to her feet. Macie latched on to his hand with both of hers, but every movement pulled another section of hair free. She tried to bury her gasp deep, but she ended up giving him exactly what he wanted. Satisfaction. Blood trickled down her nose and coated her tongue. Her teeth had cut into the side of her mouth. "You deserved much worse."

The whisper of breath tickled one ear as the killer pressed his mouth close. "Such bravery from the girl who left her friend to die."

Macie froze.

"That's right, Avalynn. I know your secret," he said. "I was there, remember? I had you right where I wanted you, but I failed to consider Hazel much of a threat. She hit me with a branch she'd found nearby.

I let you go to fight her off, but instead of teaming up on me to protect each other, you did something I was not expecting. You ran. You left her there to fend for herself. What happened next…was your fault. All these years you've been trying to find the person who hurt your friend when all you had to do was look in the mirror."

The scene played across her mind like it had a thousand times before. There hadn't been a single night she hadn't closed her eyes and known what she'd done. Hazel had come to her rescue, just as he'd said, but all she'd wanted at the time was to get away. To be safe. Tears pricked in her eyes. Not from the pain in her head or face. From the truth. She'd been a coward. Plain and simple. "You don't… You don't know what you're talking about."

"Oh, but I do," he said. "Do you want to know what Hazel's last words were? Do you want to know what she wanted most?"

Her heart threatened to beat straight out of her chest. They'd been children. No match against a fully grown man at the time. Macie had done everything she'd thought was right. She'd run home. She'd told her mother what'd happened. They'd called the police and started the search, but…it'd been too late.

"She wanted you, Avalynn. She wanted you to come back. She wanted you to save her. She begged for you until she lost her voice and couldn't scream anymore. Couldn't cry anymore." His hand lightened its grip in her hair. "Lucky for Hazel, it didn't take long for her to realize nobody was coming to save her."

The tears fell now. She hadn't told anyone. Too afraid to even admit the words to herself, but she couldn't run from them anymore. No amount of changing her name would make her forget what she'd done.

"You and I both know you deserve what's about to happen next." The hand gripped against her scalp released her hair and slid around her neck. Rough calluses scraped against her oversensitive skin. Her attacker pressed her skull back into his chest. "You know this has been a long time coming and that you belong here with me."

"Yes." She'd hidden her secret for so long, she'd almost convinced herself she wasn't that ten-year-old at all. That she was Macie Barclay, Battle Mountain PD's dispatcher. The wild woman who could read your aura, cleanse your house with sage and predict your future with tarot. The one who loved hard and fast and took what she wanted. The one people trusted and relied on. She closed her eyes as Riggs's face materialized at the forefront of her mind. It'd all been a lie. The woman he'd blindly followed into these woods didn't exist. Not really. And she hated that fact. But there was one person who knew her better than anyone. A little girl who gave the best hugs and biggest smiles. The one who didn't care who Macie was in the past, just the one who played with her, gave her unhealthy amounts of junk food and painted her fingernails outlandish colors in the present. Macie wanted to be that person. She wanted to be anything Penny needed. And right now, Penny needed her to fight.

"I deserve everything that's coming to me." Macie slammed her head back as hard as she could. The crunch of bone filled her head, and the hand around her throat released. Her attacker hit the ground, but instead of running, she would fight. She wouldn't fail Penny like she had Hazel. "But Penny doesn't. Tell me where she is, or that broken nose will be the least of your worries."

A low laugh filtered through the brush of wind in the trees. Unease flooded her at that laugh. It was a mixture of humor and victory, despite his position at her feet. "Now, what on earth made you think it would be that easy?"

His leg slammed into her shin and took her down. Macie fell onto her back. Oxygen crushed from her lungs. Before her brain caught up with what was happening, the killer was on top of her. His hands were around her throat. He was squeezing. Air pressurized in her throat, begging for release, but he wouldn't give it. It built and built until she was sure her chest would explode. He expertly used his weight to keep her in place.

Macie tried to bring her knees up, to dislodge his

hold, but no amount of bucking and wrenching deterred him. He was going to kill her. Just like he'd intended to kill her that day by the creek.

Only this time, there wouldn't be anyone to save her.

RIGGS GASPED FOR air as though the weight of an invisible hand was strangling the life from him. His skull knocked back into the tree behind him, but he couldn't move.

Vicious pain ignited through his shoulder the harder he pulled at his hands. He tried to hunch forward, to get some semblance of movement, but the thick rope around his neck constricted tighter. Any move he made cut off his oxygen supply. Blood seeped through his jacket and down his chest.

The blade was gone.

The killer must've taken it to keep Riggs from cutting himself loose. Smart. Because that son of a bitch didn't want to know what Riggs had in store for him when he got out of this mess. But the wound wouldn't stop bleeding until he was able to add pressure. Hell. How much time had he already wasted unconscious? "Macie? Talk to me, Red. You hurt?"

Where he'd expected her whiskey-smooth voice, the woods answered. Insects quieted at his added disturbance. He couldn't see much past two feet around him, but his senses were adjusting. No movement. Nothing to suggest she'd been tied to a tree nearby.

Which meant the killer had taken her. His brain automatically filled in the blanks of what that meant for the childhood friend he'd lost and for the little girl counting on them to save her. "I'm coming, ladies. I'm coming for you both."

Riggs fought against the ropes crooked in each elbow, his chest splayed wide, and the rope around his neck shifted. His scream slipped up his throat despite the pressure. Two, maybe three, more moves would silence him for good. How the hell was he going to get out of this without something to cut himself free? He settled back against the tree, and the rope relaxed.

There was only one way out of this.

But the risk of strangling himself before he got free was high.

The past forty-eight hours hadn't come to anything he'd planned. He worked missing persons cases. He investigated homicides. There was an order and a protocol to both. This case had blown everything out of the water. No. Not the case. Macie. She was unpredictable and frustrating in the best of ways. Unique and surprising. Nothing at all like he'd imagined over the years. Definitely not by the book. Her emotional honesty and creativeness outdid him at every turn. It was refreshing and scary yet somehow exactly what he'd needed on this case. And exactly what he needed to shake up his life. For a small town, he'd hated the crowded feeling Battle Mountain elicited with dense trees, claustrophobic cliffs and suffocating niceties, but she'd somehow brought out the mystery and the beauty in a matter of days.

They were here because of her. Because she knew this killer, and they were going to find Penny because of her. Her intensity and commitment to finding that girl would carry them both to the end of this sick game, but he needed to find her first. "You just gotta do it, man. They're relying on you."

Riggs filled his lungs with as much air as they could hold. He squeezed his shoulder blades together, making the rope as tight as possible against the bark. He shuffled back and forth, back and forth. The rope itself wasn't thick, but it was sturdy. He only hoped it'd gone through some wear before he'd been put in the game tonight. And that the tree bark was sharp enough to do the job.

Strands dug into his neck as he shifted and locked oxygen in his trachea. Every move burned more air, but he couldn't stop. Not yet. His shoulder screamed for release the longer he stretched the wound. He wasn't sure if the bark was doing anything, but he had to believe. Warm liquid had soaked his shirt clean through. He was either going to strangle himself or bleed out. Both final endings the killer had most likely bet on, but Riggs hadn't come this far to die in the middle of the damn woods. Becker deserved better.

The rope snapped.

Riggs took his second gasp for breath and crumpled forward. His forehead hit the dirt. He clamped a hand over his shoulder. Blood snaked through his fingers as he pulled himself together. A patter of rain started, blocking out any other signs of life. Dragging himself to his feet, he stepped on something hard. It broke under his weight. Glass? He crouched to get a better look. The shape resembled a gun, but the killer wouldn't have left Riggs with a weapon within reach. "Oh, hell."

Penny's water gun.

Macie must've dropped it after he'd blacked out.

A crack riveted along the bright orange barrel. It'd never work the same again. Riggs dug it out of the damp earth and brushed off as much dirt as he could. Holstering the toy, he stumbled down a slight incline and met up with what he assumed was the same creek he and Macie had been searching. It was impossible to tell in pitch-dark, but gurgling water navigated him upstream.

The killer had ambushed them. Which meant they'd gotten too close. Riggs braced against the arc of pain exploding down his shoulder and tipped into a nearby tree to catch his breath. Macie might've helped him see this place in a new light, but it could still kill him. He couldn't see anything out here. One wrong move could send him off the trail. "Get a hold of yourself, Karig."

Shoving off the tree, Riggs closed his eyes. Rain

punched through the canopy above and slid down his face. It was colder than the minuscule amount they saw in Albuquerque, keeping him focused and awake. He had to think. He knew this case. He knew this killer. Not as well as Macie, but close. The better part of his life had been devoted to catching this man. He knew the killer's MO and his preferences. It didn't matter he was out of his element here. The same rules applied.

Recover Penny and Macie. Take their attacker into custody.

Riggs opened his eyes and took a step forward. He couldn't rely on any footprints out here. The rain was already destroying the evidence. But he could listen. Insects were still buzzing beneath the patter of rain. He kept the creek on his left, ensuring he didn't venture too close. "All right, you son of a bitch. Where are you?"

He wasn't sure how long he'd walked. Seconds. Minutes. Nothing had changed but the feel of dirt turning to mud beneath his feet. He had to be close to the source of the creek now, closer to the lake. But it was quieter this far up, even with the onslaught of rain. The woods' inhabitants were hiding, avoiding being heard here. Riggs slowed. A hint of smoke tickled the back of his throat. Burning wood. But it wasn't the same odor that seemed to engulf Battle Mountain after the forest fire. This was lighter, fresher. A campfire?

Brushing his hand against his holster, Riggs reminded himself he'd been stripped of his weapons, but that didn't mean he was defenseless. He stepped to his left, losing the scent, and set back on course. The harder the rain fell, the faster the odor died in the air. He was running out of time. And so were Macie and Penny. He picked up the pace. Branches and pine needles scratched at his exposed skin. His legs burned as mud suctioned his boots to the ground. He was close. He could feel it.

A clearing spread out in front of him. Riggs kept to the tree line as the outline of a pop-up tent took shape straight ahead. The camp couldn't have been more than a few hundred yards from the creek. He and Macie had to have walked right by it without noticing. How was that possible? Lightning flashed overhead, highlighting the setup for a fraction of a second. A single tent and a fallen log. No signs of Macie, Penny or the killer. Riggs took a tentative step into the perimeter.

Something caught on his bootlaces, and he froze.

He crouched, reaching out. Thin wire threatened to snap, leading in both directions. "Trip wire."

This wasn't a regular camper on a vacation for the weekend. This was exactly what Riggs had been looking for. A nest. Question was, had it been set to keep intruders out or victims in? Riggs had the feeling the killer had considered both. Straightening, he maneuvered over the line and took his first step into the camp.

The fire he'd smelled was quickly losing strength under the downpour. Embers cast dim orange light in a halo around the pit. One chair, one tent. No vehicle in sight.

The girls weren't here.

"Damn it." Had he been too late? Was this all that would be left behind once the killer moved on? Riggs crossed to the tent and ripped back the front flap. An adult-sized foam pad took up most of the space in the center with a few folded sets of clothing in the corner. A small folding table stood at one side. A backpack consumed his attention a few feet away. He grabbed for it, before hauling the zippers down. An emergency pack. First aid kit, compass, windbreaker—it all looked well used. He shoved the pack back into place. Nothing suggested Penny had been here at all. If the killer was the only one in the tent, where had she been held since this morning?

The answer solidified in his gut. Riggs turned back to the log stretching from one side of the camp to the other. "You've got to be kidding me."

Rounding back into the center of the camp, he then set his hand on the top of the fallen log. It'd been gutted over the years, hollow in the center. Making it easy for the killer to install a chain on either side. Riggs picked up the links glimmering with help from the fire embers. The bastard had kept her here. Out in the open. Chained like an animal. Rage—unlike anything Riggs had felt before—exploded behind his sternum. The killer had chosen this spot. Had prepared to take another victim. Everything here testified of premeditation and intelligence far greater than they'd assumed over the years.

Riggs wound the chain around his forearm and braced his boot against the log. He ripped the chain free, sending splinters of wood in every direction.

Right before a scream cracked through the night.

Chapter Eight

His scream rang in her head.

She kneed the killer in the groin a second time. His hands released their hold around her neck. She rolled through the mud to put some distance between them. But not fast enough.

The killer grabbed on to her ankle. Macie kicked as hard as she could to get him to let go, but he dragged her back. Fingernails scratched down the backs of her legs, setting her skin on fire. Her elbow knocked into something solid and heavy. She pried it from the mud as rain pummeled into her face. Slamming the rock into the side of his face, she scrambled out from his grip. Her lungs worked overtime as she ran. Every step got her farther away from Penny, but she couldn't do anything for the girl if she was dead.

Macie darted through the trees. Her head pounded in rhythm to her racing heart, but she couldn't stop. A branch cut across her cheek and tangled in her hair. It hurt, but a few strands were nothing compared to the fist against her scalp. She wasn't sure how far she'd run. Not far enough, but flashes of that day she'd run twenty-five years ago infiltrated the present. She'd left her best friend behind to fight a killer alone.

And she was doing the same thing now.

Her energy drained the harder she pushed until she couldn't force herself to take the next step. Rain pitted against her exposed skin as she relied on a large tree to keep her upright. Out of breath, every cell in her body screaming for her to get away, she sobbed through the terror and grief.

She had to go back.

She had to find Penny.

She had to find Riggs.

She was the only one who could bring them home.

Macie swiped the water from her face with the back of her hand and looked down the path she'd run. There was nothing but darkness and pain waiting at the other end, but she'd run long enough. It was time to take a stand. "And cross your fingers you don't die in the process."

She took a full breath and backtracked through the woods. It was dark. It was raining. She had no idea if this was the right direction, but sooner than she expected, she came to the small clearing she'd woken in.

Only it was empty.

He'd already vanished.

Macie spun in circles. Maybe she had the wrong location. Maybe he was still close by. "No. No, no, no, no. Penny!"

"Macie!" That little voice cut through her fear and took up residence around her heart. Air crushed from her lungs. She hadn't expected to ever hear that voice again. Penny was close. "Macie, help me!"

"I'm coming! I'm here!" It was a trap, a way to lure her back into the spider's web, but Macie didn't care. As long as they were together, they could fight. They could go home. She slapped at trees and leaves getting in her way. The thick taste of diesel from somewhere nearby settled on her tongue, and she ran with everything she had.

A pair of small headlights lit up the woods and gave away the ATV's position. It was only then she heard the growl of an engine.

The backs of her thighs burned as she hauled herself over a boulder and through the trees. She didn't gauge the distance. She didn't think twice. Macie launched herself at the ATV and tackled both riders to the ground. The handlebars rammed into her side as Penny's scream pierced her ears. Seconds slipped by as she tried to get her bearings. "Penny, run!"

A fist rocketed into her rib cage.

Unimaginable pain ricocheted through her torso, but all she cared about was protecting Penny. She'd take a thousand punches if it meant the four-year-old could get away. Penny disappeared into the trees. She just had to keep the killer here long enough for her to get away.

He got to his feet, now standing over her. Rain pummeled down onto her face, hiding his. The ATV's headlights darkened his features from behind, but she recognized him for who he was: the monster who'd killed Hazel. "You shouldn't have done that, Avalynn."

She blinked against the downpour. There was no way out. No way she could beat him, but she'd give Penny all the chances in the world to escape. Because she wasn't that scared little girl anymore who only cared about her own survival. She'd become someone else entirely. "That's not my name."

Macie fisted two handfuls of mud and threw them in his face. Thrusting her boot into his shin, she dropped him to one knee and slammed his head against the side of the ATV. She climbed to her feet and ran after Penny. Trees ripped at her jacket and hair, but she wouldn't stop. Not until they were both safe. And Riggs… He was a trained Albuquerque homicide detective. She'd come back for him. She wouldn't give up.

A shadow stepped directly in her path.

But her momentum was too great. She couldn't slow down. Macie collided with Penny's small frame. Wrapping her arms around the girl, she tried to keep her weight off her as they hit the ground and rolled down an incline. Rocks stabbed at her back and legs as Penny's cries drowned out Macie's breathing. She crashed into a boulder twice her size at the bottom and let Penny go.

The four-year-old scrambled out of reach but then knelt to brush her small hand against Macie's face. "I'm sorry, Macie. I didn't mean it. I dropped the water gun you gave me. I'm sorry."

"It's okay. I've got you." Of all the things to be worried about, Penny had chosen the loss of a toy. Macie checked her jacket where she'd sworn she'd stored the bright orange water gun, but found warmth spreading across her side instead. She tested the stinging pain. Not rain. Blood. Her breath shuddered as she considered the chances of them getting out of these woods alive, of not bleeding out, of being able to protect a child that wasn't hers. Macie pressed herself to sit up and wrapped her upper body around Penny's. "You know what, we're going to get out of here. You and me. I'm going to take you back to your mom and dad, and we will get you a new water gun. Okay?"

Penny nodded at the same time a sliver of lightning stretched across the sky. "Okay. Can it be purple this time?"

"I think that's a great idea." She didn't know how bad the wound was or how long she had. Didn't matter. Keeping Penny calm and getting to safety. That had to be her goal. "Are you hurt?"

"My arm hurts." Penny presented her forearm where something had scraped a long line from elbow to wrist. Most likely during their fall. No other significant bruises or cuts as far as Macie could tell. She'd gotten to Penny in time.

"We'll get you fixed up in no time, slugger, but for now, we need to keep moving. That means running and staying quiet. Think you can do that?" She glanced up the hill where the ATV's headlights cast a spread of white light through the woods. She'd bought them some time, but Macie doubted the man who'd taken Penny gave up easily.

"Yes." Penny got to her feet. "If you hold my hand."

Macie clamped a hand over her side. A twig had penetrated through her shirt and embedded deep into muscle. She lowered her voice, all too aware how easy it would be for an experienced woodsman to find them. "Awesome. And when we get you back home, you can eat all the ice cream you want. My treat. Any flavor and toppings you want. You name it."

"Chocolate." Penny looked up at her in excitement. "And strawberry!"

"Shhhh. We gotta be quiet, remember? We don't want the bad man to find us." She pressed her hand against the wound, and the world tilted on its axis for a moment. She could do this. She would do this. She might not be the chief of police, a former Green Beret or a bomb technician, but getting out of tricky situations was a Macie Barclay specialty. She led Penny through another grove of trees. No telling which direction they were heading or if there was anything on the other side, but the farther they got from the killer's last known position, the better. They were going to make it. She had to believe that. There couldn't be any other option. Not for Penny.

Thunder rolled overhead, and Macie picked up the pace.

Penny tried to keep up, but her legs just didn't move as fast as Macie's. At this rate, they'd never make it to help.

A splinter of wood cracked from nearby.

Macie pulled them to a stop, then picked Penny up. Her wound screamed for relief, but they'd run out of time. "Hang on tight. You hear me? Don't let go. No matter what, and I won't let go, either. I promise."

Penny whimpered.

"And here I thought we were becoming friends, Penny," a voice said from behind.

Macie spun to face him and backed away one step at a time.

His outline advanced, countering every move. "I told you the rules, and you gave me your word you would follow them. It's a shame you're going to have to be punished for that now."

"You'll never lay another hand on her." Macie's voice revealed the terror cutting through her. She wouldn't let go. She'd never let go. Her heel caught on a root clawing up through the forest floor, but she only held on to Penny tighter. "Or anyone else."

That same low laugh that'd punctured through her confidence as he'd strangled her filtered through the trees. "You know what I like about you, Avalynn? You never give up. You never stop fighting. That's what's going to make your death so very sweet."

"Stay back." She didn't have a weapon. She wasn't trained to fight, but she did have a little girl to protect, and she'd do whatever it took to get her out of here.

The killer took another step. "Who's going to stop me?"

"I am." A second shadow separated from the trees and swung a hard right hook. The killer dropped to the ground as Riggs looked at her and Penny over his shoulder. "Get her out of here!"

MACIE RAN WITH Penny in her arms.

"I hear you like picking on little girls." Riggs shoved his foot into the killer's gut. He stretched his shoulder back and ignited an indescribable amount of pain. "Wait until you see what a real fight looks like. On your knees, hands behind your back. You're under arrest."

"Your distraction technique won't work, Detective Karig." The man at his feet raised his face to the sky, but it was still too dark to identify anything familiar. "I'll never stop, and you can't protect them both. You'll have to make a choice. The girl or Avalynn."

The swipe of a blade cut through Riggs's jeans and into skin. He jumped back to avoid the next strike as the killer shoved to his feet. The knife whined as it aimed for his midsection. Riggs blocked the attack but was too slow to see it for the diversion it was. A fist slammed into his face and knocked him off-balance. His boots slid in the mud, and another arc of pain slashed down his spine. His scream ricocheted off the trees as he hit the ground and rolled. He didn't have the chance to catch his breath.

The killer launched himself forward, blade angled down to stab Riggs through the gut. He dodged the assault a split second before the knife sank deep into the ground. Riggs turned in time to land another punch to the bastard's face, but it wasn't enough. His attacker blocked the next, twisting Riggs's hand until it threatened to snap.

"And here I thought you were offering a challenge." The killer shoved him beyond the tree line.

Riggs rocketed into a tree but managed to thrust himself away just before the blade struck again. The guy moved faster. Faster than he'd expected. This wasn't a run-of-the-mill killer they'd been hunting. No. This was something so much worse. Something experienced and deadly. "And here I thought you were some kind of formidable villain."

"Well, Detective, you haven't seen anything yet." A knee thrust into his chest and pinned Riggs back against the tree.

Pressure unlike anything he'd felt before consumed the oxygen in his chest. He launched his fist out in a vain attempt to get it to stop and hit nothing but air. His heels dug into the earth, but the son of a bitch who'd taken Penny was all that kept him upright. Complete control.

Was this how Hazel had felt in her last moments? Was this what Sakari had gone through? He'd followed in Becker's footsteps to find Hazel's killer, but he'd found himself at the same end instead. Burnt out with nothing to show for years of work. Somewhere he didn't belong. And alone.

"How does it feel, Detective? Knowing you've spent your entire life chasing me, only to realize you were never enough to help them? That you're not even capable of helping yourself." The pressure on his chest increased until a white blanket encroached on his vision.

His head was pounding. His lungs begged for relief. Riggs wedged one hand against the killer's knee to try to release the pressure and stretched one hand out for something—anything. His fingers grazed a tree branch, and he latched on with everything he had. The last reserves of air were consumed by his holler. The branch detached from the tree, and he swung as hard as he could.

Contact released the weight on his chest. Riggs sucked in as much air as he could take. The killer fell to the side. But not for long. His attacker got back to his feet, but Riggs was faster this time. He secured both hands at the base of the branch and swung up. The end connected with the killer's chin. A guttural groan drowned the pitter of rain as he hit the ground. A pair of headlights coming from above highlighted the man's outline, but it was still too dark to make out much of anything else. Riggs nearly doubled over but held on to the branch. Just in case. "Like I said. You're under arrest for the kidnapping of Penny Dwyer, for the murder of Kevin Becker and for being a straight-up dick."

"All right, Detective. You win." The killer raised both hands as though in surrender.

Instinct warned Riggs it shouldn't have been this easy. Still, he couldn't deny the sense of victory charging through him. It was over. Twenty-five years of interviewing witnesses, crime scene reenactments and searching. It'd all led to this. To Hazel's killer. To Macie's attacker. To Penny's abductor. "On your knees, hands behind your back."

The killer lowered his chin to his chest, doing as he was told. "Whatever you say."

Riggs had no warning.

The blade stabbed deep in his thigh, and he dropped to one knee. His scream stretched far and wide through the trees as disbelief caught him in the moment. Blood seeped into his jeans and trickled down into his boot.

The man in the shadows pulled the knife free, before lowering his mouth to Riggs's ear. "Just as long as you can drag me out of here yourself." A low laugh penetrated through the ringing in Riggs's head. The killer stood, then shoved Riggs onto his back. "Not up for it? I don't blame you."

Rain peppered across his face. Cold and hard. Adrenaline escaped his control as he lay there bleeding out. He had to get up. He had to fight. The bastard at the other end of the knife wouldn't stop gunning for Penny. For Macie. Riggs was the only one standing between a killer and them, and hell, that little girl deserved more than a life on the run and full of fear as Macie had. He could give that to her. He just had to get up.

"The more you fight, the worse it gets for you, Detective." The outline above him limped forward, headlights gleaming off the slick blade in his hand.

"That's what I tell my girls. Some listen. Some don't. I hope, for your sake, you don't make the same choice as your partner."

His girls? Those two words penetrated through the pain and the dizziness and scraped him out from the inside. The victims this man had killed weren't his. He didn't get to keep them like trophies. He didn't get to think back on them fondly and congratulate himself for a job well-done. Riggs summoned everything he had left and launched himself off the ground.

He hiked his wounded shoulder into the bastard's gut and shoved him back into the same tree he'd been pinned against. Riggs went for the throat, but two fists slammed down onto his forearms and broke the hold. He took a gut-wrenching hit to the ribs. Once. Twice. Again. Pain exploded from each strike and left him unstable and out of breath. He blocked the oncoming right hook, but he wasn't prepared for the left.

Lightning struck behind his eyes. Blood filled his mouth and gushed down his throat. Shoving back, Riggs battled to catch his breath.

"You know, it's funny. Your partner… What was his name? Becker." The killer sucked in a deep breath from a few feet away. "He warned me about you. Said I'd signed my own death warrant. That I had no idea what I was bringing down on myself. And here you are." The shadow crouched beside him. "I'd have to say, I'm not impressed."

"How about by me?" That voice. *Her* voice. It cleared the haze from his head and gutted him all at the same time. No. She wasn't supposed to be here. "Run."

Macie swung a large branch into the killer's head.

The killer turned to face her. He took the full force of her swing across the face and dropped to the ground, out cold.

"Macie? What...what are you doing?" Riggs scrambled to kick the blade out of the man's hold, before sending it flying into the brush. Pain arced through his thigh. He needed something to tie off the wound before he bled out. "Where's Penny?"

"Just over there." Macie reached for him. Soft skin colliding with his as she gripped him under one arm and hauled him to his feet. "We heard you scream. Couldn't leave you to die alone out here."

"No." This wasn't right. She couldn't be here. She was supposed to take Penny and run. He tried to push her off. "You have to get out of here, Macie. Go. Now."

She refused to budge, her grip tight on his arm. "Riggs, you're hurt. You're bleeding. Let me help you—"

"He's never going to stop." Riggs dragged her into his chest. Didn't she understand? This wasn't over. As long as the man who attacked her all those years ago was alive, this wouldn't end. "He'll never stop coming for you or for her. He used me to bring you back here. He's..." He looked back to keep the killer in his sights. And froze. "Where is he?"

"What?" Macie's grip lightened on his arm. "He was... He was right there. He couldn't have gotten up without either of us noticing."

That was exactly what the son of a bitch had done.

Riggs's heart rate rocketed into his throat. Hell. He scanned the trees.

A scream pierced through the night.

"Penny." Macie dropped her hold and ran into the tree line.

The killer couldn't get far on foot. Riggs headed for the incline as a shadow crossed in front of the ATV's headlights. He clawed through slick mud and despondent root systems. The wound in his leg protested every step. The growl of an engine filled the trees. Then the odor of diesel. Just like he'd smelled at Macie's home. He was going to lose them.

"Penny!" The girl's name tore up the back of his throat. He'd lost the feeling in his fingers and toes. He'd lost too much blood. He'd lost the only shot he'd had of ending this. He couldn't take another loss. Riggs found a foothold and pulled himself onto solid ground.

The ATV fishtailed through mud and deeper into the woods, brake lights lighting up the trees. Too fast.

Macie broke through the trees to his left and ran after the trail left behind. "No!"

He grabbed Macie around the waist to keep her from following. It wouldn't do any good. Not anymore. They were beaten. They just hadn't accepted the truth yet.

Penny's voice trailed back to them and settled in the pit of Riggs's stomach. "Macie!"

Chapter Nine

She should've gone after the ATV.

Macie winced as the nurse swiped an antiseptic pad across the cut along her side. The wound wasn't deep. They'd been able to get the twig out in one piece. No splinters. The lights were too bright here. Everything was so sterile. Like a morgue instead of an emergency room. Her head hurt, and she was pretty sure she'd cracked a tooth, but none of that compared to the emptiness inside.

Penny was gone. Again.

They'd been so close to bringing her home, but Macie had failed. She'd let her out of her sight mere seconds too long. Just enough for the killer to steal her right out from under her care. Tears burned in her eyes.

"Does something hurt?" The nurse took a step back, studying every inch of Macie's exposed skin not covered by the flimsy gown.

Her entire body hurt, but it was her insides that

couldn't take the damage of what'd happened. What was she going to tell Campbell? What would she say to Kendric? After all the years of not knowing his daughter, the former ATF instructor had only been allowed a mere few months with her. That wasn't long enough. Macie shook her head. "No. I'm…fine."

The small clinic in the center of town was equipped to handle minor injuries, concussions and broken bones. Not so much teeth. She'd have to see Dr. Corsey for that. As for Riggs, she wasn't sure where he'd been taken. He'd collapsed after they'd lost sight of the killer's ATV. The stab wounds in his thigh and shoulder had caused him to lose too much blood too fast. She'd done what she could to stop the bleeding, but her destructive nature insisted it hadn't been enough. That she'd never see that lopsided smile or get to reminisce about some stupid thing they'd done as kids. The downward spiral of grief and anger and hurt she tried to ignore intensified. He'd been innocent in all this, but he'd gotten too close. She tried to warn him. She certainly hadn't been enough to save Hazel or Penny. How on earth did she convince herself she could've saved him, too?

"All done." The nurse discarded her gloves in the trash bin and reached for the clipboard on the small table beside the bed. "Looks like you got lucky. Just some minor scrapes and bruises. You'll want to keep ice on that jaw up to twenty minutes. Then I'll come back with your discharge papers and a set of scrubs you can wear since the police took your clothing."

Macie wasn't entirely sure she'd heard everything. Her mind was someplace else. On someone else. "Have you… Have you heard anything about the man I came in with? Riggs Karig? He's a detective. He was stabbed during the struggle."

"I'm sorry. Unless you're family, I can't give you any information. I'll be back in twenty minutes." The nurse closed the curtain around her bed. If only it were that easy to shut out the world.

Macie held the ice pack to her face. Family. That single word had been blurred over the years. Of course, it'd started with her parents, but even then, Hazel and Riggs had become something more than friends. And here, in the middle of nowhere, the men and women she'd sent into the night after killers and bombers and gunmen, on searches and evidence collection and into interrogation, had crossed the line she'd drawn between them.

She'd tried. She'd tried to distance herself and keep them safe in case the man who haunted her nightmares returned, but deep down, she didn't want to be alone. She was tired of moving town to town, of changing her name and settling for people believing what they wanted about her. She couldn't think of a single person in all these years who knew her for who she really was. But in Battle Mountain, she'd made mistake after mistake, letting them in.

Letting Penny in.

Then Riggs.

Two days really wasn't enough time to get to know someone, but they hadn't just met, had they? He'd known her since before she was ten years old. The real her. The self-conscious, misunderstood and moody woman she'd always been. And, still, he hadn't walked away.

She might've gotten him killed, though.

The curtain parted, and the face she couldn't seem to get out of her head came into focus. Riggs. He was here. He was alive. On crutches but alive. Hallelujah. "You look like you got in a fight with a bear."

Macie dropped the ice pack from her face and buried the urge to smooth her hair as she shot out of bed. One step. That was all there was between them, and she closed it as fast as possible. Encircling her arms around his neck, she accidentally rammed him off-balance. One of his crutches hit the floor and claimed the attention of nearly every nurse and physician in the vicinity. She pressed herself to him, hoping to provide him a bit of support, but mostly to convince herself this wasn't a hallucination. "You're alive."

"Not if you keep strangling me like that." Riggs didn't move to pry her free. As though he might've needed the contact, too. Just for a little while.

His warmth penetrated through the thin gown and chased back the effects of the ice pack. She didn't know how long they'd been at the clinic. Hours based on the sun peeking through the window, but he looked more put together than she did. And showered. Macie loosened her hold and lowered onto the soles of her feet. Rubbing at her face, she studied him up and down. "Could you have at least tried to put your face in front of his fist or something? Looking at you makes me feel like a dirty punching bag."

"You look beautiful." That lopsided smile was back, and Macie felt the need to sink into his arms. "Your backside waving in the wind and all."

Embarrassment checked her fast as she jerked to collect both sides of her gown in the back. Only to realize the stainless-steel instrument cart on the other side of her closed-in area had given him a full view of her rear end. "Forgot about that part."

"It's not every day women are that happy to see me." Riggs couldn't seem to keep from smiling, and the tight knot in her chest gave her a bit more room to breathe. "You've set the bar quite high."

"Glad to add a bit of flair to your life." Her attention was back on that smile. On the split in his lip. Without thinking, Macie trailed her thumb over the laceration. "How bad is it?"

He set his hand over hers, that intense gaze softening on her. "The blade went through a good chunk of flesh. Lucky for me, it didn't hit anything major. Not having time for leg day the past few months has paid off. Few stitches, and these bad boys have got me covered." He tapped the remaining crutch. "My shoulder is another matter. Good thing I'm a righty."

"I'm sorry." She didn't deserve to have a few moments of laughter after what she'd done. To him and to Penny. Macie pulled her hand back, instantly cold again. "For all of this."

"Don't do that." Riggs framed one side of her face with his free hand. "You and I both know there was nothing we could do for her in our condition. We fought for her, Macie. We bled for her. She knows that, and she knows we will not stop looking for her. We're not done."

"He said Hazel begged for me to save her before she died. That she died thinking someone was coming for her." Memories of last night—of the terror and desperation in Penny's voice—fed into the growing hollowness in her chest. Like a piece of her had been stolen. "That's all I can think about. Penny out there, cold, restrained, crying for someone to help her. I had her, Riggs. I had her, and I let her slip through my fingers. I knew what would happen if I left her alone again, but I... I couldn't let you face him alone. What kind of person does that make me? Leaving a four-year-old to fend for herself."

"Hey." Riggs wrapped her in his free arm while keeping balanced on the crutch. "You had an impossible choice to make, and because of you, I'm standing here. You saved my life, Mace."

Mace. She liked that. The way he seemed to accept not just her name, but the person she'd been hiding deep down. The one who'd run the moment she'd gotten a chance twenty-five years ago. The one who'd spent that time trying to make things right and who'd inadvertently brought Penny into danger. "I don't know what he'll do to her now. The other two victims had three days each, but Penny tried to escape him. She almost made it. He's going to punish her. Because of me."

He'd spent the same twenty-five years trying to fix what was broken with Hazel's case, but Riggs couldn't fix this. No matter how much she wanted him to.

"He won't go back to his campsite. It's been compromised. Your interim chief has already dispatched the entire department into those woods. They're tearing apart his camp inch by inch." Riggs rested his chin at the crown of her head, fitting her against him. Perfectly. Like a puzzle that'd been waiting for its partner. "They'll find something to tell us where he might've taken her. Until then, we have the knife he threw at us at your house. Ford didn't recover any fingerprints, but it's custom. Someone will recognize it."

Confidence never came easy to her, and she sure could've used some of his right then. Battle Mountain PD had been built from the ground up with a collection of determined, insanely capable and caring individuals from all areas of law enforcement.

Coroners, former military, ATF, state investigators, district attorneys—people who had made their mark on the world long before they'd helped this town. But Macie… She wasn't any of those things. Actually, she didn't know what she was, but Riggs looked at her as though she were important. Like she could do something to bring Penny home. "What now?"

"Now we get you dressed and the hell out of this place." He gave her one last glimpse of that smile before tugging the curtain closed behind him.

She clamped her hand back to the opening in her gown. Right. Because she was still naked as a jaybird under this damn piece of fabric. "And then what?"

"Then we find out where the son of a bitch who took Penny is going," Riggs said. "And you and I bring her home."

THIS PLACE WAS worse than the motel.

He wasn't sure who the hell had thought it was a good idea to buy a run-down cabin in the middle of the desert, but it hadn't been a good one.

The floorboards protested with every step. Dust had congregated on every surface, and Riggs was pretty sure those were bullet holes in the wall.

"It's not much, Karig, but it'll do. This place isn't on any map. Isla's husband made sure of it." Adan Sergeant took up more space in the dilapidated postapocalyptic kitchen than anyone else. At well over six-foot-six, the former sniper was not easy to hide.

"We planned on fixing it up and moving out here, but Mazi insists on being part of every design decision, and so far, those decisions include a whole lot of pink, purple and glitter. No one will look for you here."

The man was right. It wasn't much, but all he needed was a place for him and Macie to keep a low profile for a couple days. Just long enough to get their bearings after nearly dying in the middle of the woods. Riggs pressed his thumb into a hole almost the size of this thumb. A sniper bullet. Something had happened here. Recently. "You're married to Isla Vachs, one of Ford's officers?"

"That's the dream, man." Adan slapped Riggs on the back, and he nearly coughed up a lung. "I'm sure you know what it's like. The incessant waiting for the right time, the planning. Hell, I don't even know if Mazi wants me as a dad."

He caught sight of Macie crossing the hallway at the back of the cabin, and his entire system lit up in awareness. That was all he'd felt since they'd left the clinic. A connection as though his body knew exactly where she was at all times. He hadn't ever felt that with his wife. Back when they'd gotten together, getting married had just felt like something they were supposed to do after dating for five years and some months. Both of their families had expected it, and neither of them had been getting any younger. Turned out, that wasn't the best way to ensure a healthy marriage. It'd all started falling apart when he'd spent more time with his nose in Hazel's case file than with his wife. Riggs had just...made her disappear. Long before the divorce. "Yeah. I know how that feels."

"I've stashed some weapons under these floorboards and in the cabinets. Just in case." Adan motioned to a few key locations. "Isla had me put in an alarm system, too. Anyone or anything comes onto this property you aren't expecting, you'll be prepared."

"You expecting trouble?" He'd trusted BMPD's newest recruit and his—whatever Isla Vachs was—with Macie's life at her insistence, but how well did he really know these people? Protocol dictated local PD take jurisdiction on any crimes in the town boundaries. That didn't mean they were on the up-and-up, and it didn't mean they had any clue as to what they were doing. Not like big-city police.

"Always." Adan Sergeant straightened to his full height, and one thought settled at the front of Riggs's mind. Anyone stupid enough to take on a former sniper protecting his family, his property and his town deserved whatever came for them. "We take care of our own out here, Riggs. We don't have anyone else."

With that, the military man nodded goodbye and closed the front door behind him.

"Did Adan give you the 'we take care of our own'

speech yet?" Footsteps registered from down the hallway, and Riggs turned in time to catch Macie wipe a bit of dust from her high-waisted slacks.

It was part of an ensemble she'd pulled from that duffel bag she insisted on retrieving from his hotel room. This whole place was covered in dust, but it looked damn good on her. Although the mint green color of her pants was bound to give them away if they had to make a run for it out here in the desert. Still, they accentuated the shape of her hips, the clench of her waist. The dresses had complemented her personality, but the slacks and tank top combination put everything on a whole other level. All he could think about right then was running his hands along several inches of creamy smooth skin.

Her voice graveled to mimic Adan's as she flexed both arms. "'We don't have anyone else, Macie.' I swear all the man thinks about is where the next bullet is coming from. He's pretty, though."

Riggs forced himself back into the moment. "Makes sense. Seeing as to what him and his partner went through. Especially with an eight-year-old in the mix."

"Yeah." Macie swiped ChapStick across her mouth. The movement hollowed one side of her face and exaggerated the head wound. A small butterfly bandage pulled two sections of skin together at her temple. The killer had done that, had hurt her the way he'd always intended, and now he had someone else to take all that anger out on. "No way to live, though, is it? Looking over your shoulder all the time. It gets exhausting."

She would know. Riggs memorized the notches where Adan had marked each cabinet and floorboard. One for each weapon the soldier had hidden. Smart. Riggs imagined that hadn't just been for himself but for Isla, too. The way Adan had talked about fixing the place up, how their eight-year-old wanted to be involved in all the design decisions—Adan Sergeant wasn't miserable with his choice. "He seems happy. As exhausting as constantly worrying about what threat comes next can be, I'm sure it makes you appreciate what you have. Pushes you to live in the moment."

Macie slowly capped her ChapStick and slid it into her pocket. "Yeah. It does. Makes you realize what you don't have, either."

His instincts said they weren't talking about Adan Sergeant anymore, and Riggs hobbled to close the distance between them. Damn crutch was bruising the underside of his arm, but the other option was crawling on his hands and knees. And he wasn't even sure he could do that. He lowered his voice, catching a quick shrill of wind through one of the windows. "What is it you think he's missing out on?" Riggs tried to hold her attention. "He's got a partner, a girl who has him wrapped around her little finger, a job protecting the people of this town. What more could he want?"

Her voice sounded small as she crossed her arms. A protective gesture, one meant as armor against this line of questioning, and it was then he had his answer. This wasn't about Adan. This was about her. "A job—relationships—is well and fine, but without purpose, what good is it? What good is any of it if you don't know who you're actually meant to be?"

Meant to be? Riggs studied her a moment longer, and understanding hit. He took the risk of stepping another inch closer. All these years, he worried about following in Becker's footsteps rather than leaving some of his own. Of leaving a legacy behind after he was dead and gone. He'd at least had a guide. Someone to show him the ropes and give him the choice of what kind of man he wanted to become. But Macie... She'd never had that chance. "You've spent twenty-five years on the run out of survival. A man attacked you and intended to kill you, just like he killed your best friend. You didn't have the time or the mental capacity to figure out purpose or who you are."

"I felt safe here. For the first time in years, I felt safe," she said. "That's why I stayed so long. I've been in Battle Mountain for six years, Riggs. During that time, I've watched the officers in the department risk their lives for each other and this town.

I've seen them fall in love and start families and live entire lives from behind my desk. They're out there doing the hard things to ensure every single person in this town has the same opportunity, and what am I doing? I'm on the sidelines. I'm answering phones and tracking down Greta Coburn's husband's urn for the thousandth time because teenagers ran off with it after she locked it outside on the porch. Or I'm making a run to Caffeine and Carbs for the chief like I'm some damn personal assistant or babysitting one of these hellions locking themselves in the drunk tank." She was out of breath, her shoulders rising and falling in erratic rhythms. "This…this isn't a life, Riggs. This isn't me."

Riggs dragged her against his chest with his free hand, inhaling that hypnotic scent he'd associated solely with her these past few days. Delicate and sensual. One hundred percent Macie. Her hands spread across his lower back, her head resting against his heart but careful of his shoulder. Right where he needed her. Where she belonged. Because despite the pain of her leaving all those years ago, she was the one holding them together. "Then tell me what it is you want, Red."

"It doesn't matter." She pulled away. "Penny is out there. We're no closer to finding where the killer took her than we were yesterday, and Campbell and Kendric need my help more than ever."

Riggs didn't let her get far, his hand trailing down the back of her arm.

"It matters to me." And it did. Somehow over the course of this investigation, Macie had become something more than his childhood friend. More than a potential witness. More than a victim. Just... more. What she felt, what she had to say, it mattered. Dozens of cases had taken their toll on him, had hardened him in ways he'd never imagined. But in less than a week—out of his comfort zone and faced with the failings of his past—she'd left her mark. Something permanent and irrevocable. Even if he went back to Albuquerque tonight, a piece of her would stay with him.

She didn't answer right away, to the point he wasn't sure if she would. "I want to be happy. Is that too much to ask? To just have one moment of unfettered joy without worrying where the next threat was coming from." Macie set her hand over his chest. "To feel something real and honest and exciting. I know it can't last forever. I know it's stupid when I'm stuck in the middle of a case, but I want—"

Riggs captured her mouth with his.

The momentum maneuvered her back into the wall ridden with bullet holes. Her hands fisted in his collar, pulling him closer, and his heart rate rocketed to keep up with the desire pulsing through his veins. Heat speared down his spine and into his gut so fast he had to catch his breath. Staring down at her, he tried to gauge her reaction. "Is that exciting enough for you?"

"I'm not sure." A smile tugged at one corner of her mouth. "Let's try it again."

Chapter Ten

That...hadn't been part of the plan.

At all.

Her body ached in all the places she'd forgotten could pleasurably ache. Battle Mountain was a small town. There were only so many rides she could take on the merry-go-round of eligible men and come back for seconds, but none of them had compared to the detective who'd blown her pity party out of the water last night.

Macie brushed a thin layer of dust off her face as she opened her eyes. Ugh. It was everywhere. Her hair, her teeth, up her nose. It'd take days to get it all out. This place was dreadful. And exactly what she and Riggs had needed.

"Good morning." Riggs lay across from her, wide awake, as though he'd been waiting for hours. Probably had in order to look like he'd stepped fresh from the shower. Did the man ever show signs of mortality?

Macie sniffed his damp hair and pressed a hard

finger into his muscled chest. A chest she'd gotten to know very well over the past few hours. Because, she had to be honest, when was she ever going to get the opportunity again? "You showered, didn't you? You used all the hot water so you could wake up next to me looking like that. How dare you."

"Well, I mean, you compared me to a masterpiece a couple days ago." He motioned down the length of his body, the lower half hidden beneath the same sheets she clutched to her chest. The movement cost his shoulder, though. "I had to hold up my reputation. Who knows how long this is all going to stay in one place?"

Wind whistled through the cracks in the window seal and forced a veil of glittery sand into the sunlight. It could almost be romantic. If they hadn't been relegated into shacking up in a literal shack. Grittiness exfoliated her arms as she tugged the sheets higher. "And to think, I was going to let you have your way with me again. Now I'm thinking you're going solo."

Her confidence waned as she got a full memory of what'd happened between them last night.

"Well, where's the fun in that when you have the real thing right in front of you?" Riggs maneuvered closer, that intense gaze locked on her. At the time he'd cuffed her to her own steering wheel, she'd been uncomfortable with that perceptive focus. Now she couldn't seem to look away. He tilted her head back with his thumb braced under her chin, his hand cupping her neck. Her skin started itching where he touched her. The bruising around her throat was still sensitive, but he was careful. Planting a kiss there, he lit up every cell in her body until she was practically shaking. "What if I apologized?"

She gasped as he nicked her throat with his teeth and nearly collapsed back against her pillow in surrender. Who was she kidding? He'd given her the greatest gift her soul craved: peace. And there was no way she was giving it up so soon. Not after years of living on the edge of survival. "I'd say too bad. You should've saved me some hot water."

"Mmm." The vibration of his voice reverberated all the way through her. Riggs angled his uninjured leg between her knees. "I'm sure I could keep you warm in there. Or maybe we could share once the tank heats back up."

An echo of Penny's scream pierced through her mind. Macie stilled, any semblance of desire lost. Riggs had done exactly as he'd promised. He'd made her forget the horror that'd followed her all these years and given her a reprieve, but he couldn't make it go away entirely. That was impossible.

Riggs pulled back. Humor evaporated, replaced with concern. That same hand that'd exposed her throat to his mouth angled her face down so he could look at her. "Hey, tell me what you're thinking."

"I…" She didn't know what to say at the possibility of losing the only semblance of quiet she'd felt in years. She'd had an entire lifetime of misery and fear. Couldn't it leave her alone for this?

"You can still hear her, can't you?" His gaze dipped to her mouth, then back up. "Penny."

That invisible guard she liked to keep close pulsed in defense. Impossible. Last time she'd checked, he hadn't been able to read her mind. "How did you know that?"

"Because I can hear her, too," he said.

A new wave of appreciation flooded through her and pushed tears into her eyes. Macie secured her arms around his neck, their bodies fitting one against the other. Days of uncertainty, terror and pain fled in an instant. Until all that was left was the man in her arms. She'd convinced herself no one would ever understand her. That no one had gone through what she had, but if there was one person in this world who even had an inkling, it was him. Riggs knew her past and gave her permission to be herself. Not the alias she'd constructed. She wasn't alone. She never had been. She just hadn't realized what it would take to find her way back to him.

Or who would've had to die.

Macie buried her nose in his neck, trying to steal a bit of his warmth for herself. "We need to find her, Riggs. Before it's too late."

"I keep my promises." He rested the side of his head against her chest, right over her heart, and she swore the battered thing tried to reach him with how hard it pounded. "I intend to see this through. No matter what it takes."

She skimmed the back of her bruised and scraped knuckles along his jaw. Bristled hair—softer than she'd expected—tickled her oversensitive skin. It was amazing to think of what'd changed since he'd shown up on her doorstep. She'd wanted nothing more than to get out of Battle Mountain and away from him as fast as possible. He'd been a boulder in her way and a reminder of a past she wanted to forget. Now, after everything they'd lived through, she realized Riggs might be the only one who could get Penny through this. The only one who could get her through this. Because it wasn't over. "Thank you. For everything."

"I'm just glad I cuffed you to your steering wheel. Otherwise, who knows where we'd be." His fingers grazed the scar running down her back, like he was trying to memorize the shape. His rumbling laugh shook through her and loosened all the tension and kinks from falling asleep beside someone who took up more than half the bed.

"Right. About that… I'd say it's time for some payback." Macie shoved him off of her as hard as she could.

He disappeared over the side of the bed and hit the floor with a loud thud. "Hey!"

"Oops." She kept the sheets for herself. Daring a

peek over the edge of the mattress, she checked to make sure he hadn't torn any stitches and got a full view of the magnificent specimen that'd chosen her to cavort with last night. Still a masterpiece, even with a couple stab wounds. "Forgot you can't catch yourself. Sorry."

Riggs climbed to his feet with the help of the nightstand. "Just for that, I'm eating whatever Adan stocked in the pantry. All of it."

"Be my guest. I can already tell you what you're going to find. Mazi's favorite food is Pop-Tarts, and that man has no problem giving in to her every whim." She pressed her back against the headboard as he rounded the end of the bed, the sheets still clutched around her. He limped, rubbing at his shoulder. "Looking good, Detective. How about a spin?"

"How about I take these with me?" He ripped the sheets from her grip, leaving her exposed in every sense of the word. Tying them around his waist, Riggs disappeared through the bedroom door. "Pop-Tarts, here I come."

"This isn't over!" Macie scrambled to cover herself with the pillows he'd left behind. Her laugh escaped her control but died just as quickly. Oh, hell. Pressing the pillows against her, she sat up in bed. It wasn't about how far he'd go to find Penny or what'd happened between them last night. It wasn't about his attempt to learn as much as he could in order to be ready for threats, his intensity when he looked at her or that he could read her better than anyone else. The banter, the jokes and teasing, and connection they shared…

It was all of it. And she wanted more.

For the first time she could remember, she wanted to get close to someone. She wanted Riggs to know her, inside and out. She wanted to wake up like this every morning with someone keeping her warm and happy to see her. She wanted to know him. His likes, favorite foods, if he watched sports, the women he'd been with. Every scar, mistake and regret. She wanted it all. More importantly, she didn't want to run anymore. Not from him.

Living at one extreme end of the emotional spectrum had made her highly sensitive to changes in her mood, especially given she hadn't allowed anyone to influence her or get close. But these past three days… They'd blindsided her until she wasn't sure which way was up.

Macie tossed the pillows and gathered her change of clothes from the floor. Muscles she didn't even know existed cramped, and she fell into the side of the mattress with a *humph*. Her side stung a bit, but it was nothing compared to what she'd put Riggs through last night. "Now, this is just ridiculous. Pull yourself together, woman."

It wasn't like she'd never been interested in a man before. She'd gone through dozens, but this one hit differently. Did something funny to her insides, which didn't make sense. She and Riggs were friends. It wasn't like he was going to stick around Battle Mountain after they closed this case because he'd gotten laid. It wasn't like they had a chance together. He'd go back to Albuquerque and solve more homicides, and she…

Didn't know what she was going to do.

Macie lowered herself onto the edge of the bed, Riggs's question loud in her head. What did she want? It'd been easy to answer him last night because a moment—or a couple hours—of bliss had been exactly what she'd needed to break from the past. But life didn't come with never-ending orgasms and men willing to provide them on a whim.

The nightmare that'd followed her for most of her life was finally coming to an end. She could feel it— the killer closing in.

She just hoped she was strong enough to face him the next time.

RIGGS TOOK ANOTHER bite of stale pastry.

Macie had been right about the inventory in the pantry. Who the hell lived off of Jolly Rancher-flavored breakfast pastries? He dropped the rest onto the paper plate he'd found and shoved it away. What he wouldn't give for one of the donuts from Caffeine and Carbs to wash out the aftertaste.

His attention slid to the hallway where movement registered from the bedroom at the back. Or someone to help get rid of the taste. Phantom sensations prickled in both hands. Silky hair fisted between his fingers, curves of creamy skin at his command, a sharp exhale against his fingers—it all worked to make him forget the past three days. Last night, wrapped up in Macie, feeling her become part of him, had given him a focus he hadn't experienced since the start of his career. When he'd had a purpose. Every case he'd worked had always come with a question at the back of his mind. It didn't matter if it was a homicide, a missing persons investigation or a burglary. That single question had remained the same in each instance.

What would Becker do next?

The man had guided him into the department and through the ranks from the time Riggs had been ten years old. Help with homework in high school, advice on college essays and which courses would fast-track him into the department, pop quizzes and bloody dioramas built from homicide cases Becker had worked in the past. All in an effort to turn Riggs into the detective Hazel McAdams deserved on her case. A hint of PTSD flared at the thought of all those mornings Becker had broken into his apartment with a bullhorn to start Riggs's day off with a five-mile run. "You don't get to run my life anymore, old man."

But if there was ever a moment he needed Becker, it was now.

This case… It was important. He couldn't afford

to screw this one up. He'd convinced himself finding who'd killed Hazel had been solely for her family. To give them peace of mind and a way to move forward. Now he realized they hadn't been the only ones hurting all this time.

He needed to do this for Macie. And for Becker.

Riggs pulled Becker's case file in front of him. His mentor had combined the McAdams and Vigil cases into one file. He'd broken protocol, but the late detective wouldn't have done it without good reason. *First rule of homicide investigation, kid—keep your file clean. You can't solve a murder if you can't find your damn notes.* Becker was a better detective than that, so there had to be a reason these two cases ended up together. Then again, for all Riggs knew, Becker was having his own brand of petty revenge by making a mess for Riggs to sort through.

The wound in his thigh pinged as he shifted closer to the table. Riggs had sifted through every note, every report, and separated them into two separate piles. He'd studied Hazel's case backward and forward for years. He recognized the investigative plan and crime scene photos and made quick work of dividing those pages into their rightful place. As for Sakari Vigil's case file, it was all fresh. Anything that didn't match up with Hazel's murder went into the other pile. He'd gone through the entire folder in a matter of minutes. As he and Macie had already concluded, there were no notes conveying why Becker had come to Battle Mountain, how he'd known the killer had come here or why his body had been found in an abandoned building. It was as though an entire section of the file had been taken, leaving them at a dead end. Riggs leaned back in the chair.

This was what living in his partner's shadow for so long had gotten him. Dead ends, no new leads and three unsolvable cases. He'd never had a chance. All those cases he and Becker had worked, the old man had taken the lead, had come up with the plan and had narrowed down a suspect. And Riggs... He'd just been along for the ride. A tourist. He wasn't a detective. He was a fraud, incapable of solving a single case on his own. He was going to end up just like Becker. A has-been, a joke to the department, forced into early retirement. And Penny Dwyer would be the one to pay for his mistakes. "Hope you're proud, Becker."

His phone vibrated with an incoming email. He scrubbed both hands down his face and flipped the screen upright. Becker's preliminary autopsy report. He'd missed the exam, but considering he'd been trying to stop a killer from strangling two victims at the time, Riggs couldn't feel anything more than mild regret. He skimmed the first couple of pages. "Multiple bruises around the neck, defensive wounds on the hands and forearms."

The scene played out in his head in full color. Becker hadn't gone willingly. He'd fought. For his life, for the victims'. In the end, his partner had believed he was the only one who still cared about Hazel's case. He'd known the risk of pursuing the investigation, and it hadn't stopped him. *You have no idea what you're bringing down on yourself.* Wasn't that what the killer recalled Becker had said in his final moments? Even at the edge of death, his partner had believed in him. Had believed Riggs would do the right thing and take this thing to the end.

"You had to have known what you were getting yourself into." He discarded his phone on the table and went back into the case files. "Come on."

He scanned through each handwritten note, over and over again. Names of neighbors from the canvass at both scenes, interview notes, theories written down, then scratched through. He and Macie had been through all of it at least a dozen times in the motel. And none of it was getting them anywhere. His attention drifted back to his phone. To the autopsy report of the one man he could credit for getting him out of the hellhole where he'd been raised. Becker had had his faults, but he'd been everything Riggs had needed in the end. The old man wouldn't leave him hanging now.

Riggs dragged his phone closer, reviewing the photos taken of the body. Becker had let his beard get out of hand, more gray than the dark brown Riggs recognized. Few more wrinkles, too. Hell, his partner had aged a matter of years without anyone noticing. Least of all him. Didn't change anything it seemed. Becker was still wearing sweaters under suit jackets. Riggs battled the urge to look away, but his partner had trained him to take in every detail.

Even the ones that didn't seem relevant...

Like a rash Riggs had never seen before. He pinched the screen to make the photo bigger. There. Just under Becker's left cuff at his wrist. Red splotches stood stark against the paleness of his partner's skin. He closed the window and went back to the report. A rash would be documented in the autopsy report. His heart beat faster as he searched through any marks discovered on the body at the time of the exam. He needed a better view of the reaction.

"Please tell me there's coffee." Macie swept into the room and headed straight for the pantry to start the search. She'd be sorely disappointed unless her favorite food matched that of an eight-year-old. His gut clenched as he caught sight of her in high-waisted slacks that showed off her figure. Having her this close alone was enough to shove reality back a few seconds, but then Riggs noticed the red marks along the side of her neck. Not bruising. Something else.

"What's that?" He shoved to his feet, making sure to take the sheets he'd stolen from her with him. Angry welts pimpled in a cluster near her throat. They weren't like the mosquito bites he'd suffered from the woods. These were like blisters. "You've got some kind of rash."

"Oh." Macie covered the area with her hand. "I've been scratching."

His mind instantly tried to connect the two instances. Becker came into contact with the killer, as did Macie. In fact, the rash seemed to follow the same pattern as the bruises darkening around her throat. "Does it hurt?"

"It itches. Happens sometimes. It's just an allergy I've always had. It's nothing. They'll go away in a couple hours as long as I leave them alone. Kind of like hives but smaller and more annoying." She continued pulling the mountain of stacked boxes of lime green breakfast pastries from the shelves. "Okay. I promise I was joking about the pastries. Is there seriously nothing else to eat?"

Riggs pushed her hair back behind her shoulder to get a better view, exposing the affected area. "I didn't notice them last night. What are you allergic to?"

"Peanuts." She tossed one of the boxes back into the pantry. "Riggs, I promise, I'm fine. This is the worst it gets. I've had in-office allergy tests every year to keep on top of it. I'm not going to go into anaphylactic shock, and I don't need an EpiPen. Stop worrying."

"Does this kind of reaction happen a lot?" he asked.

Her eyebrows crinkled in the middle. "No. I'm pretty good about staying clear from anything with peanuts. You'd be surprised how much food contains nuts. They're everywhere. Even these things." She tossed a box of pastries back in the cupboard and closed the pantry.

"Becker was allergic to peanuts." He wasn't sure of the relevance to the case or how it would lead them to recovering Penny, but it was a lead. Something to tie the man they'd fought in the woods to both attacks. "His body was found in a burned-down bakery. No amount of peanut residue could've survived that fire, which means the killer had to have had it on his hands when he killed Becker and attacked you."

Macie rubbed at her neck as if suddenly conscious of the fact she'd been strangled a little more than twenty-four hours ago. A shiver chased across her shoulders. "Makes sense. Direct contact with allergens can produce the rash."

"He's not going to hurt you again, Macie." Riggs stepped in close enough for a hint of soap and clean woman to tickle the back of his throat. "It doesn't seem like much, but this is something new we can focus on."

"You want to hunt a man who has peanut residue on his hands. That's not exactly a telltale marker of a killer, Riggs. Plenty of people handle peanuts in their jobs or to just snack on," she said. "What are you going to do? Have an allergist test everyone in town?"

She was right. It was an impossible task to follow. "Then we're back at square one."

"Maybe. But if there's one thing I know about you, it's that you don't give up. Even when the chips are down and you're bleeding out." She ripped the sheets from his hand and crumpled them in her arms, leaving him completely and utterly exposed to the elements. "Now, if you'll excuse me, Detective. I need to wash these."

Macie sauntered back down the hallway.

Chapter Eleven

She couldn't stop scratching her neck.

Macie shoved her hair out of the way to get a better view in the small bathroom mirror. The rash was getting worse. Damn it. She hadn't lied when she'd told Riggs it usually went away within a couple hours. What was this? Super peanut? Didn't matter. A rash wasn't going to help them find the killer, and it sure as hell wasn't going to help them find Penny.

Their best shot was going back through Becker's files, but they'd already done that. Ad nauseam. Penny was smart. Her parents taught her to beware of strangers and all the other rules of interacting with a scary world. She wouldn't have gone with a killer willingly just like Macie hadn't gone with him all those years ago. She would've screamed, fought, bit, punched—anything and everything she had to do to get free. She would've let Easton know she was in danger.

Unless…she hadn't been able to. Unless she'd

been knocked unconscious or drugged or restrained. The killer had twenty-five years to get his skills up to par. Because of her. Hazel, Sakari, Penny—they'd all been taken. But she could still help one of them.

Macie stared at Campbell Dwyer's name in her phone contacts, her thumb hovering above the entry. She feared for what waited on the other line, but they'd already wasted so much time Penny didn't have. She'd taken refuge in the bedroom as Riggs reviewed his partner's files from the beginning. She couldn't just stand there. She had to do something. She pressed the screen and raised the phone to her ear. The call connected almost instantly.

"Do you have something?" Campbell's voice shook, tearing through Macie with every quaver. The pain was real and suffocating and uncomfortable, but ignoring it wouldn't make it go away. Shoving it deep down only made things worse.

"No. I just…" She wasn't sure exactly why she'd called. The seconds stretched between them, like she and Campbell had somehow become strangers overnight. Macie rubbed a clammy hand down her slacks. Didn't help her nerves in the least. "I wanted to see how you were doing?"

"How I'm doing, Macie? Really?" A humorless laugh staticked from the other side of the line and sucker punched Macie in the gut. "My daughter has been abducted for a second time, you're hiding instead of out here with us to look for her, and you want to know how I'm doing?"

The attacks just kept coming. Macie closed her eyes. Hiding. The word took up so much space, it was hard to breathe. She had been hiding. Not just since the attack in the woods. But practically her whole life. She'd looked at Hazel from the sidelines, all the while protecting her own skin. Because she was afraid. For her life, for what she'd find, for the people she cared about. She forced herself to take a deep breath and keep the emotion lodged in her chest from breaking free. "Someone has to. Have you eaten or gotten any sleep the past couple of days?"

Campbell didn't answer right away, didn't even seem to breathe, but she hadn't hung up. It wasn't much, but it was progress. "There will be plenty of time to sleep when I find her."

Her pulse thudded hard in her throat. Thoughts that'd been circling her brain for years rushed into focus. She'd lived this exact moment every time she'd opened the closet where she'd hidden the pieces of Hazel's investigation she'd collected. She knew everything going through Campbell's mind. Every fear, every hope, every justification—it'd all been leading to this moment. To someone else taking up the mantle, and her being able to walk them through it. To keep others from having to do it alone as she had. Tears burned in her eyes. "It wasn't my fault, Campbell."

"I…" A deep inhale registered. "I know that, and I'm sorry. I'm sorry I blamed you. I just feel so…"

"Helpless." Campbell and Riggs were similar in that respect. Macie glanced toward the door, not hearing anything from the kitchen table anymore. He must've given up on the files. Or fallen asleep. Neither of them had gotten much rest over the past few days. "I know it feels that way, but I promise you are a good mother. I see you with Penny. I see how she looks at you and how far you were willing to go to get her back that first time. You almost died bringing her home, Campbell. How many other mothers would've gone up against a psychotic killer to protect their child? I know for a fact you're in the middle of the woods right now, searching for her, trying to kill yourself all over again."

A crunch of leaves confirmed her theory. "I can't stop, Macie. I can't go home. No matter how many times Kendric tells me I need to take care of myself or that I need to eat or get some sleep, I can't do it. Because I know the second I do is when she'll need me the most."

The duffel bag she'd carted from her tree house consumed her attention from the corner where she'd dropped it the night before. The files inside were still there. She'd double-checked. Hazel had been her best friend, and still, all these years later, that need to keep going, to find the next lead, to do something worth doing, gripped her hard. "They're going to tell you that you can't do anything for her unless you take care of yourself. They're going to have the best intentions. They're going to try to make you see reason. Screw reason, Campbell. Don't listen to them. Eat a granola bar, take a power nap in your car, then get back out there. If it's permission you're looking for, you have it from me. Penny needs you, so suck it up, buttercup, and focus on her. Let us take care of everything else."

The silence was back. Just for a moment. "I'm glad I didn't have to kill you."

A smile notched her mouth higher. "Me, too. Good luck out there. I'll check in with you as soon as we have news."

The line disconnected, and she stared down at the phone. The timer she'd set to run in the background was still ticking down. Forty-eight hours had somehow diminished in the blink of an eye. Now they had less than twenty-four to find Penny.

Movement registered from the doorway. Riggs.

"It's not polite to eavesdrop, you know." Macie tried to force a smile as the weight on her chest increased, but she was tired of carrying around all the facades she'd relied on over the years. For once, she just wanted to be. No expectations from others. No internal compulsion to stay bright and cheery and reliable.

He moved into the room, all predatory-like and smooth, carrying a grace she'd never had. Taking a seat beside her on the bed, Riggs let his arm settle against hers. "You told Campbell exactly what she needed to hear. You're good at that. Reading people."

"I've always wanted a superpower." His warmth added to the sensation overload closing in but soothed the raw edges of the past few days at the same time. "Maybe next I can start reading minds."

"You were one of the kids in chemistry who ignored the safety rules to see if you'd turn into a superhero, weren't you?" he asked. "Mixing up things the teacher told you not to, just to see what would happen."

"You know me so well." Her laugh took her by surprise. It was so easy to forget the world existed outside of these four walls with him here next to her. As though twenty-five years had been a blip of time, and they'd picked up right where they'd left off. "Did you find anything new?"

"I've gone through Becker's autopsy report and called in to your interim chief. Easton and the rest of the department are all hands on deck, but nothing at the campsite we uncovered gave them anything. Every printable surface had been wiped down. Same with the knife we recovered. I'm beginning to think the killer made it himself. It was like the bastard had known we were coming." Riggs shook his head. "Did you happen to catch the model or license plate of the ATV while you were out there?"

"No. It was too dark." She tried. She'd gone over

those terrifying minutes again and again, but nothing new had come to mind. They were still dead in the water, and Penny was drifting farther out to sea. "I couldn't even pick out a color, to be honest, and trying to track one of those will be like trying to find a needle in a haystack. Everyone who owns property around this town has them to help work the land."

"Last I heard, Ford was calling in some favors to the surrounding departments, trying to get as many boots on the ground as possible," he said. "Your guy Reagan from the coffee shop has even volunteered to keep everyone hopped up on caffeine and pastries. Whole town's involved now. The killer can't last out there forever."

"And what if he's not out there?" Ice slid through her veins. "What if he's already done with her? What if what we did out in those woods pushed his timing? He'll just move on to the next town and do this to someone else. We can't sit around and wait for news, Riggs. We need to do something."

"You were strangled twenty-four hours ago, and I lost two pints of blood the last time we went up against this guy." Riggs set one hand against his thigh. "If you've got a plan that ends with who we're after in cuffs, Penny on her way home and us still alive, I'm all for it."

That was a tall order but one they couldn't walk away from. All that mattered was bringing Penny home safely. Whatever it took.

"Come with me." Macie shoved off the bed and rounded back into the living space. The kitchen table was still covered with files, now separated into two distinct cases. Hazel McAdams and Sakari Vigil. "Look at the photos of the victims." She pointed to the first photograph, unable to bring herself to study them again. It wasn't Hazel and Sakari she saw anymore. It was Penny. "The only marks found on their bodies during the autopsy were the strangulation bruises."

"Okay." Riggs didn't sound convinced of anything yet.

"He's preserving them while holding them captive." It was a long shot, but they had nothing else to go off of. "He's being careful with them, making sure not to damage them in any way until the finale. I don't have proof, but I know for a fact Penny wouldn't have gone with a stranger willingly. She knows what her parents do for a living, and they taught her everything she needed to know to fight back, but he wouldn't have wanted to knock her out or sedate her because that would leave a mark."

Riggs picked up that first photo and took another look, clarity and determination spreading across his face. "If that's the case, he would've had to convince her to leave with him. How?"

Macie hated the theory that'd taken hold, but it was the only one that made sense. "I think Penny knew her abductor. I think she went with him willingly."

WILLINGLY. THAT WAS a big leap.

But if Macie was right… If Penny knew her abductor…

Hazel could've known hers. Sakari could've looked into the face of a man she trusted while slowly suffocating, all the while believing he would loosen his grip. That left Macie. She'd been the killer's original target all those years ago, hadn't she? He'd gone after her first. Would she recognize the man determined to keep to the shadows?

The primal need he'd tried to ignore when it came to this case had returned with a vengeance. He couldn't pretend anymore. He couldn't turn his back. He had to see it through to the end. He had to know who'd done this. Too many people had died from his refusal to acknowledge the truth. Innocent lives. That was on him. Which meant both Penny's and Macie's lives were on him.

"You're chasing a damn ghost, Karig." Riggs scrubbed a hand down his face. A rise of frustration powered through him, and he shoved the stack of cases off the table. The papers scattered into a mess of blurred words and stark images. Every other homicide he'd worked had left a trail of clues for him to follow, even on the tailcoats of Becker's career. There'd been evidence, motive—something— he could use to find the right answer, but this case… It wasn't like the others. This killer wasn't like the others.

A washed-out photo of Becker on the slab had landed on top of the rest from BMPD's investigation file, separated from the preliminary autopsy report. The final wouldn't come through until the case was closed. *Second rule of homicide investigation, kiddo—don't make it personal.* A scoff escaped his control. Too late for that. This was personal. Every inch of it. He'd known the first victim and the last. They'd both played an integral part in shaping him into the man sitting here with nothing but a handful of crime scene photos and a witness getting under his skin. He collected the photo from the scattered pile. "You knew I'd come running, didn't you? You knew I'd do whatever it took to see this through. Because that was how you trained me."

The hole he'd tried to fill with case after case collapsed in his chest, leaving nothing but hollowness and grief. His eyes burned. Why hadn't Becker retired like he was supposed to? Why couldn't the man have found a hobby or traveled the world in an RV like everyone else his age?

The answer solidified as the seconds ticked by.

Macie.

Becker had wanted to find her. To help her. To protect her as he hadn't been able to protect the others. And when he couldn't—when he'd died trying—his partner had trusted him to take up the cause. He'd come to Battle Mountain in a last-ditch effort to save lives, and instead, had lost his own. Doing what he loved.

Riggs tried to rewrite their last conversation in his head, but there was no getting around it. He'd accused the old man of controlling his career from the get-go, but in reality, Becker had led him here. To Macie. "You always were trying to set me up on dates."

"You know there are doctors who can help with the voices in your head." Macie settled against the wall beside the hallway—the same spot where he'd kissed her. Damp hair waved down her shoulders, curling in the front and waving in the back. Hints of citrus and something compelling and rich. He'd smelled it on his pillow a few hours ago when he'd woken beside her, and instantly imagined falling asleep with that same scent on him tonight. "Personally, I think mine are more interesting than the people around me."

Riggs memorized everything he could about her. He could still taste her, feel that perfect mouth beneath his, and there wasn't a single cell in his body that wanted to stop him from doing it again. He could get used to this. Despite the case that'd brought them together, Macie had blown his organized and routine world apart, and he didn't miss a single moment of it. In as little as three days, she'd given him a renewed energy he hadn't felt since graduating from the academy. A fresh outlook. She gave off a light when his entire life had become dark and lonely. It wasn't just about saving lives anymore. It was about living his own. Doing as she had done in choosing her own path, looking out for the people she cared about and staying curious. "The only voice I have in my head these days is yours."

"You say that like it's a bad thing," she said.

He shifted his weight into his good leg and stood, closing in on her. His uninjured hand found her hip as though it'd been carved just for his touch. Full, soft and enticing. "Took some getting used to, but now, I can't imagine it any other way."

"I've heard I have that effect on people." Macie wound her arms around his neck, lighter over the patch of gauze and tape on his shoulder. "None as handsome as you, though."

Hell, she was beautiful. Vibrant. Confident in all the right ways. His total opposite. Maybe everything he'd been missing in his life. Somehow, even in the middle of all the violence and terror and uncertainty, she'd become a lighthouse directing him through the dark and doubt. He needed her. Today, tomorrow and the day after that. Longer if they could manage it. There wasn't anything or anyone waiting for him back home he wasn't willing to give up right this second. For her. He fit her against him. Absolutely perfect. "How do you do it, Red? How do you manage to make things look so effortless and easy when the world wants nothing but chaos and challenge?"

"Practice makes perfect." Macie seemed to test the words for a few seconds. "But nothing is as easy as it seems."

Her answer lacked that sarcastic and lighthearted flair he'd come to associate with her. Riggs loosened his hold to get a better read of her expression. "What do you mean?"

"I wasn't always like this, Riggs. These past few years, on the run… I used to know who I was. I didn't have to lose myself in things like astrology or fifteenth-century plants, and read any book I could get my hands on, hoping something would light a spark," she said. "I think that's one of the reasons Easton Ford doesn't know how to talk to me. No one in this town knows how to talk to me. To them, I'm the airheaded dispatcher preaching her voodoo and giving herself manicures at her desk. But the truth is, I don't know what I'm meant to do on this planet and that scares me. So, yeah, I guess that I might make this look easy, but that's because I have no idea what I'm doing. I'm lost."

Lost. The word snaked through his mind and settled at the forefront. It was an uncomfortable feeling. All this time he'd relied on Macie to get them through this investigation—to lead him in the right direction—and it turned out, that confidence he'd acquainted with her didn't exist. But the longer he looked at her, the longer he had her in his hold, Riggs knew one thing for certain.

"I know who you are." He pushed a strand of damp hair back behind her ear. "I'll admit, I was confused there for a while. The stubborn girl I knew twenty-five years ago was still stuck in my head. Avalynn was powerful, confrontational and never liked anyone telling her what to do. She only cared about one thing. Being in control. Everything was a test of wills, especially when it came to her best friends. But it's never been clearer to me than right this second, Macie Barclay. You're not her."

She moved to argue with him.

"You're sensitive to everyone else's needs but your own. You're willing to put yourself in harm's way for the sake of a four-year-old girl and a burned-out detective who'd rather be in the desert than the woods." Riggs smoothed his thumb along the seam of her blouse at her side. "You're the most self-aware and honest person I've ever met and able to take the lowliest situations and make light of them. The world needs that. I needed that." He took another step into her, her chest pressed against his. "You're creative, and intelligent, and feisty in the best of ways, and I can't imagine going back to Albuquerque without that light you bring in my life."

Her mouth parted on a sharp inhale. "What…what are you saying?"

"I'm saying when this case is closed—when Penny is home safe and the man who took her is behind bars—I want you to come back with me. It's taken me this long to figure out all these years, I haven't just been looking for Hazel's killer, even Becker's killer. It's you, Macie. I've wanted you back in my life since the moment I realized you'd left." Pain registered from his leg, but he pushed it to the back of his mind. He'd stand here on a bum leg for a hundred more hours as long as Macie waited at the finish line. "I came to Battle Mountain to make up for a mistake, but Becker's death is more than one of a hundred homicide investigations I've worked. It's a chance to start over. For both of us."

"Wow. I don't know what to say." Her tongue darted across her bottom lip. "I've been thinking about that question you asked me. About what I want. I built a life here. I have friends here. For the first time in years, I think I've made a home, and I don't want to lose that feeling." His gut checked him hard as hesitation contorted her features. Those wide green eyes locked on him. "But I've also never felt closer to another person than I have with you, and I've missed that connection."

"I'm not going to try to convince you one way or another." That would be a losing battle, with him as the sore loser. "It's your choice. Not mine, but know I'll accept whatever decision you make."

"I've already made my choice." Her full-blown smile nearly knocked him on his rear end. Macie launched onto her tiptoes and fused her mouth to his. Before he had a chance to fully enjoy the taste of her again, she dropped onto her feet. "But if I'm going to come back to Albuquerque with you, if we're really going to give this a chance, there's something you need to know first."

"What is it?" he asked.

"That day with Hazel in the woods." Her voice dipped into a whisper. "Everything I told you was true, but I didn't tell you the whole story."

Confusion cut off his air supply for a second. "What else is there to tell?"

"Hazel came to my rescue when the killer grabbed me, like I told you, but I lied when I said I didn't remember much after that," she said. "I remember everything."

Chapter Twelve

The admission should've lifted the weight off her chest, but Riggs hadn't responded yet. Her heart rate notched higher the longer silence reigned. "Say something."

His hand faltered on her hip as he took a step back. That unreadable guard was back in place, and the warmth charging through her veins at his proximity cooled significantly. She didn't know what was going through his mind, but it wasn't every day a witness came forward to recant their story.

"Okay. You'd said he asked you for directions, right before he attacked you. You didn't get a good look at his face because he surprised you from behind. You remember Hazel hitting her killer with a branch to get you free." Riggs released her entirely. No longer comforting or supportive. He was back in detective mode. Unreachable. "What happened after that?"

"I ran. Down the mountain." She could still feel

the wet spots on her shirt where Hazel had hit her with clumps of moss. They'd crusted the longer she'd run. Macie clenched her hand into a fist to keep from testing her blouse for the same stains now. "I don't know for how long. I looked back to make sure Hazel had followed after me, but she wasn't there. Once I saw his face, I just ran faster."

And the truth was out. Her shame and her guilt right along with it.

"Wait. Now you're saying you saw his face? And you…didn't tell anyone?" Horror widened his gaze, and everything went cold. "You said you couldn't identify her killer. That you didn't remember anything distinct about him."

"I lied." Those same words had played through her head thousands of times. They'd kept her up at night, followed her into every friendship she'd tried to build when she took the risk and driven her to take a meaningless job for the smallest police department in the country. But coming from him… They cut deeper than she'd ever imagined. "You have to understand. My parents were convinced I was next, that he would come for me, and that fear became a part of me. I lived with it for days. I couldn't sleep. I couldn't eat. I refused to leave the house or be alone. I didn't know what else to do."

"It sounds like you did, Macie. It sounds like you could've given police a chance to catch Hazel's killer, but you chose to save your own skin instead." A hardness she'd hoped never to witness again solidified across his features. "What if your account could've helped Becker solve the case? What if Hazel's family could finally have the answers they deserve, and you were the only person keeping them from moving on? Hell, Sakari Vigil and Becker might still be alive if you'd told the truth." Riggs shook his head as he backed away. "All this time, you could've done something, and you chose to stay silent. That's not the kind of woman I want a relationship with."

Dread pooled at the base of her spine. Macie locked her jaw to keep the tears from burning in her eyes, but it was no use. She'd known this day would come—the one where someone saw her for what she truly was. A coward. She just hadn't expected it to hurt this much. "I made a mistake. Okay? I should've told you, but I lied because I wanted you to see the real me. The one you said you wanted to come back with you—"

"I was wrong." His voice lost any semblance of emotion. He'd detached faster than she'd expected, leaving nothing but a shell of the man she'd fallen for. Dark eyes assessed her every move, seemingly seeing right through her. "You haven't changed, have you, Avalynn? You're still that girl who only gives a damn about herself."

Avalynn. He'd stopped using that name over the past few days. He'd accepted her as who she was now, not who she'd been. At least, that was what she'd told herself. Hearing it now severed the connection they'd shared and left her empty and wanting. Macie rolled her lips between her teeth and bit down. It was the only way to keep the grief and heartbreak from tearing her apart. She leveled her chin parallel to the floor, trying to hold her ground. "I'm not that person anymore."

"Could've fooled me. Then again, you're good at pretending to be someone you're not." Riggs stared at her as though wishing he could take it all back. The night they'd spent together, the support and promises he'd let slip through that intensity he carried—it'd meant nothing to him right then. Now facing toward the door, he walked over the mess of files and grabbed his keys off the counter.

The killer was still out there. He knew Riggs now. He couldn't just leave. Macie moved to stop him. "You can't go. It's not safe."

Riggs pivoted on her, and she pulled up short. His anger centered on her and destroyed the remnants of feeling in her veins. "Lucky for me, I can take care of myself. Unlike Penny. Someone has to have her best interest at heart."

"Didn't I try to do that the other night? Didn't I try to save you, too? You don't know anything about me, Detective, or how far I'll go to bring that girl home." If he was going to try to erase their time together, she would, too.

"You're right. I don't. Whose fault is that?" He wrenched open the door, his limp more prominent then. "I'll let your department know where you are. Until then, do what you do best, Macie Barclay. Look out for yourself."

The door slammed closed behind him.

After a few seconds, Macie flinched as dirt kicked up against the windows during his escape, leaving her alone. Without a vehicle. Without support. Another layer of dust cascaded down from the exposed rafters like a wall of glitter. It got under her collar and made her itch. She grabbed at her neck, aggravating the rash along one side. "What the hell is happening?"

She hadn't eaten peanuts, and even if she had, the reaction should've calmed down by now. Unless...

Unless this wasn't a food allergy as she'd assumed.

Macie tore her gaze from the SUV speeding across the desert landscape. Riggs had said something about Detective Becker being allergic to peanuts, too. She dug through the papers strewn across the floor until she found the photo focused entirely on the rash at the man's wrist. It looked the same as hers. That was impossible. Everyone reacted to allergies differently. What were the chances the rash would show the same pattern? "He had it on his hands."

Not peanuts. Something else.

She discarded the photo, pouring herself into the case and not the ache growing bigger in her chest.

Riggs was gone. He wasn't coming back here. Not for her. The only way she could help Penny now was on her own. "Think."

Food, medications, insect bites, latex—there were dozens of sources of allergic reactions, but none of them seemed to fit the bill now. But chemicals might. In fact, now that she thought about it, she'd heard about this kind of reaction when she'd first started as a dispatcher for BMPD, and there was only one place in Battle Mountain this specific rash could've come from. If Penny was there, they had more to worry about than bringing her home.

Macie pulled the file together and ran to the back of the cabin. Adan and Isla were survivors, and they did everything they could to protect their eight-year-old from danger. Not from diabetes, but they'd want to keep a fueled vehicle ready to go. She raced through the back door and kept on going to the newly built shed positioned between the cabin and the cliffs less than a mile away. Hauling the garage door overhead, she then rounded the fender of the monster truck parked inside. It'd been built by and belonged to Isla's late husband. Fully decked out and stocked for emergencies. "Bingo."

It took two tries to get herself behind the wheel. She shoved the key in the ignition, and she could've sworn the engine growl was about to shake her fillings loose. She shoved it into Drive, leaving the cabin she'd learned to love in the rearview mirror.

Dead Again

There was nothing to look back for. Only forward. If there was one thing she'd learned the past few days with Riggs, it was this place—these people—they were worth risking her life for. All of them. She was done running. "I'm coming, Penny."

Macie stepped on the accelerator and tore across the desert back toward town. Meeting up with the dirt road that would take her up the mountain took less than twenty minutes. The truck's shocks threatened to give out as she forced the vehicle along rocky terrain. With her luck, she'd pitch the oversize beast backward, but before any real fears set in about becoming a crash test dummy, the mouth of Desolation Mine materialized through the trees.

"This is it." She'd never come up here, but the teenagers set on making her and Weston Ford's lives miserable a couple times a year had told her everything she needed to know. The mine had been abandoned once the coal companies pulled out. Workers had started getting sick. They didn't know from what, but it hadn't been worth the investment when so few could keep digging. Macie slid from the truck, the ground unsteady. Or maybe that was just her. Mud suctioned at her shoes from the storms from the past few days. She pulled a flashlight from one of the emergency containers in the back seat and compressed the power button. The beam lit up the dirt ahead of her but disappeared into the mouth of the mine. "Here goes nothing."

Goose pimples budded along her arms as she trekked the few yards to the mine's mouth. Only darkness waited. An emptiness that felt like it could swallow her whole if she wasn't careful, but if Penny was in there, she didn't have a choice. A rock rolled under her flimsy shoe, the sound of which echoed deep into the cavern. Something shifted inside. "Please be here."

Macie let the darkness consume her. She took a step, then another. The temperature dropped the deeper she treaded. It was more humid in here than she thought it'd be. The flashlight didn't help much, but it was a reassurance to hang on to at least. Her pulse thudded hard at the base of her skull. She felt as though there were a thousand eyes watching her every move, but she couldn't see any of them. "Penny?"

She wasn't sure how far she'd gotten, but it was enough to make doubt start clawing in her head. There were plenty of spots in a place like this that weren't safe. Not just from asbestos as she feared had caused the reaction on her neck, but open shafts, collapsed areas miners didn't dare venture, gas pockets. The list went on. But she couldn't go back. Not without Penny. Glancing the way she'd come, she misstepped. Her foot hit something solid and out of place.

The thin piece of wood broke under her feet.

And she was consumed by the earth.

HE SHOULD'VE KNOWN BETTER.

He should've known not to let himself get wrapped up in this investigation. In Macie. Becker had tried to warn him about letting things get personal, but he hadn't listened. There was a reason detectives needed to keep their distance. Because the moment emotion played into a case, mistakes were made. And he'd made the biggest one of them all.

Riggs shoved the SUV into Park and hit the pavement. Battle Mountain's police station looked the same, but his entire world had turned upside down. Nothing he'd done the past few days made sense anymore. He wasn't this person. The kind that fell for a woman in three days. Who believed every word of a traumatized witness on the run, then managed to climb into bed with said witness. Macie had gotten in his head and put his conscience in a blender. Hell. She'd lied straight to his face, and here he'd been thinking about a future. With her.

Wasn't going to happen.

He shoved through the back door of the station and maneuvered down the hall to the left. The chief's office was empty, but Easton Ford wouldn't have just up and abandoned the place. Someone had to be here to answer emergency calls—

"Detective Karig." Kendric Hudson got to his feet from his position behind the dispatcher's desk. Macie's desk. Gruff facial hair shadowed a strong jaw and a path of scar tissue that immediately put

Riggs on edge. This was a man who didn't appreciate small talk or beating around the bush. No time
or patience for anything but the truth, and didn't put
much stock in anything but. Riggs had met plenty of
investigators like this one over the years, but there
was something unique. Something capable and quick
and tested. "We haven't been formally introduced,
and you seem to be missing our dispatcher."

"Officer Hudson. Good to see you again." Riggs
extended his hand, his shift in weight aggravating
the stab wound in his thigh. "And no, Macie's not
with me."

A knowing smile hiked one corner of the man's
mouth higher, but clear frustration bled into his grip
as the former ATF instructor shook his hand. "So
what was your plan, Detective? Because the way I
see it, a killer took my daughter and is using her to
get his hands on Macie. If Macie's not here, he's got
no reason to keep Penny alive. You were the one
who was supposed to make sure she didn't leave
town. That we actually had a fighting chance." Hudson advanced on him, every inch the federal agent
and father Riggs had expected that first day. "You
don't know me, Karig. You don't know my wife. You
weren't here that first time Penny was taken from us,
but I promise you, if anything happens to my daughter or Macie because you refused to follow orders, I
will not protect you from what's coming."

Plan? If he was being honest with himself, Riggs

hadn't had a plan. He'd gotten so caught up in his anger—in his disappointment—with Macie's lie, that he hadn't seen anything straight until he'd walked through the station door. She'd left Hazel to defend herself against a full-grown attacker, without looking back, without trying to help. He'd meant what he'd said. She wasn't the person he believed he'd known, and there was no changing that. "Macie didn't leave town. She's safe. As long as she stays put and you let me do my job, Penny still has a chance."

Kendric Hudson sank back against the edge of the desk, pain clear in his expression. Grief did that. Caught you off guard, made you weak. The man was in no position to contribute to this investigation or protect this town right now, but Riggs would be an idiot to think Kendric would let anything keep him down. "If you don't mind my asking, Detective, given what I know about you and Macie's past friendship, what on earth makes you believe she'll stay where you left her?"

Cold infused his veins. "She doesn't have any transportation out there in that dust bowl. Where is she going to go?"

"I haven't known Macie as long as the others around here, but she's one of the reasons I get to hug Penny and Campbell every morning and kiss them good-night after every shift. She keeps me and the people I love safe. She's unique, I'll give you that, and frustrating beyond belief at times, but she loves harder than any other person that's come through these doors. I don't care what's going on between you two or why you abandoned her to fend for herself out there in the middle of nowhere. You'd be surprised how resourceful she can be when she feels the need to help, and you'd be stupid to cut her loose." Hudson studied him as though seeing straight through into his head. "You've spent three days with her, Detective. Surely, you've seen by now she can read anybody in a matter of seconds and tell you everything you need to know about their habits, their relationships and how far they're willing to go to protect what they love."

His mind clawed to put Hudson's riddle together for himself. "Adan Sergeant was former military."

"He was. Now, from what I've heard, you're a damn good detective. You've solved more homicides in the Albuquerque PD than anyone else, including the man who mentored you." Hudson dragged himself to stand, no evidence of struggle. "Do you honestly believe a trained sniper who lost everything would leave his fiancée and eight-year-old without a way to escape that cabin in an emergency?"

Oh, hell. Gravity took what energy he had left right out of him. What had he done?

"Majors and Gregson will meet you out there." Hudson headed for the chief's office. "And might I suggest you stop wasting what little time you have to make things right. You never know when you'll run out. Take it from me."

Riggs rushed for the back door and was behind the wheel of his rental faster than he should have been with two fresh wounds. Rubber screamed in his ears as he fishtailed out of the parking lot to catch the main road. Panic strangled him at the throat. For as angry and betrayed he'd felt at learning Macie had lied to him all this time, he wasn't the type of man to let her get herself killed. They didn't have a future together, but she deserved to live the rest of her life free.

Hudson was right. Macie had never taken a command to heart that didn't suit her own parameters. That determination and stubbornness had been one of the things he'd loved about her the most, but he'd been stupid to think she'd do anything for her own good.

Loved. No. He didn't love her. Because he couldn't love someone who hid part of herself from him, who insisted on staying stuck in the past. But he'd keep his promise. He'd make sure she walked away from this alive. Just like he should've done for Becker.

Asphalt turned to dirt as Riggs skidded down the single road that would take him out past the town limits. Greenery thinned on either side of the SUV, raw dust and barren landscape stretching ahead. This was his element, where he thrived. Where he'd learned to survive. No shadows. No places to lash out from the dark.

He skidded to a stop in front of the cabin and shoved the SUV into Park. Dirt gritted between his teeth as he ran for the front door. Another car pulled up behind him, but Riggs didn't have the attention to focus on anything but Macie. Of making sure she was alive. Safe. He charged through the front door. "Macie!"

Pushing himself through the cabin, he searched every room. There was no sign of her. Their shared breakfast still waited on the table with the files he'd scattered under his feet. But something was different. The photo on top of the pile... That wasn't the one he'd been looking at last.

Heavy footprints registered from the porch. Two sets. "You Karig?" a male voice asked.

Riggs knelt on his good leg and collected the photo of Becker's wrist, inflamed and blistered. He could just make out the shape of the killer's fingers wrapping around the skin. Macie's neck had developed the same rash. The autopsy report hadn't come to anything conclusive about the source, but both Macie and Becker were allergic to peanuts. Was that why she'd dug through the photos for this? "She's not here."

He tossed the photo back into the pile and turned to face the officers at the door.

Cree Gregson took up more space in the run-down

cabin than Riggs had gauged from their limited contact at Macie's tree house. Not with his sheer size but with a heaviness that seemed to fill every inch of the place. Like he'd taken on the weight of the world and hadn't let go. The former ATF agent kept close to his partner. Protective. Devoted. Riggs knew the feeling, but the woman on his mind would never feel the same. She couldn't. "Isla keeps her truck in the back garage. The rig was installed with a GPS system by her husband before he died."

"If Macie took it, it won't be hard to track her down." Alma Majors tugged her radio from her belt. He recognized the name from a huge wave of media coverage a few years ago, but why the foremost researcher of Mexican archeology had disappeared to a town no one had ever heard of escaped Riggs. Didn't matter. All he needed was her help. "I'll hail Isla now. See if we can get a location."

There had to be a reason Macie had left the safety of the cabin. She was impulsive, but she didn't have a death wish. Even for Penny. He treaded down the hallway, ignoring the imprints of two heads in the pillows on the bed and rumpled sheets. He didn't have time to think about the rush of hours spent wrapped up in a woman who'd given him so much. The second Gregson and Majors searched this place, they'd know what happened between him and Macie. They'd know he'd broken protocol and gotten mixed up with a witness, but he'd keep the rest to himself.

As much as he hated the idea of what Macie had done, those had been the best hours of his life. For once, he'd gotten a glimpse of life outside of what Becker had created for him. He'd forgotten about the job, his divorce, the pain in his body, and he'd been able to just…be.

Because of her. He owed her that.

Her duffel bag consumed his attention from the corner. She hadn't gone anywhere without it the past few days. Why leave it behind now? Unless it wasn't useful anymore. Dragging it toward him at the edge of the bed, he then unzipped the bag. No spell books or weapons or stuffed animals from an escapade in the woods. He pulled a manila file folder from the depths.

A picture had been paperclipped to the front cover. One of three idiot kids with a hot-air balloon behind them. He remembered the day it was taken. He and Ava—Macie—had gotten into a big fight, but the balloon festival was too grand and fantastic for either of them to remember what about. He'd slung his arm around her and smiled as Hazel's mother took the photo. It would've been one of the last before their friend's body had been found.

Riggs set it aside, not daring to lose himself in that feeling all over again, and cracked the file open.

This was something far more dangerous. Familiar photos spread in a sort of timeline across the file, handwritten notes written on scraps of paper, official reports with ink smudges. It was all here. Every shred of evidence. Every witness statement. Plus her own memories. Some of these had to have been years old. Decades.

Riggs couldn't believe it. Each report looked as though it'd been tacked with a pushpin. Maybe to a corkboard or... "The closet. That's what you were hiding."

Hell. The killer had gone looking for this file during the search of her tree house because he knew. He knew Macie had been investigating Hazel's case from the beginning.

Chapter Thirteen

The flashlight beamed straight into her eyes.

Macie blinked to clear the confusion and haze, but the only thing that followed was pain. So much pain. She'd landed on her right arm. A groan echoed off the enclosed walls and reminded her where she was. It stretched the bandage on her side. Forcing her gaze straight up, she tried to make out the top of the shaft she'd fallen down. There wasn't a particle of light from above. Thankfully the shaft had run diagonal, or she'd be dead. "Hello!"

Her head protested her voice ricocheting back at her. Pushing up on her uninjured arm, she hissed at the ache in her hips and feet. No telling how far she'd fallen. Only that she wasn't getting back to the surface.

Bracing one hand against the closest wall, she climbed to her feet. Her skull struck a jutting rock before she had a chance to straighten fully. Lightning speared across her vision, and she pressed her palm against the sore spot. "Can anyone hear me? Hello!"

She'd gone down a mineshaft. No one could hear her.

The weight of that reality squeezed the air out of her chest. Her hand shook as she felt for the next stretch of wall. From what she'd studied about the mines in these mountains, shafts like this were used to get spoils to the surface, for ventilation or to access raw treasure troves. Macie collected the flashlight from the mine floor and shone it straight overhead. Considering the size of the hole she came through, she bet ventilation. Which meant it would've been man-made, right? There'd have to be an end somewhere. She just had to find it.

Then again, what did she know? She'd put her whole heart into a man who'd left her the minute she'd trusted him with the truth. She hadn't expected that, but it went to show she was right all along. No one would understand her. No one could understand what she'd gone through that day or what she'd been through the past few years. Least of all a detective who'd given up trying. Macie pressed her injured arm into her rib cage, but it was nothing compared to the hurt inside.

Riggs had chiseled past her guard with promises and support and pleasure and taken up space somewhere he had no right to occupy. Then he'd taken that privilege and used it for his own benefit. To give himself permission to push her away. Just so he could go back to his comfort zone, to being alone. Macie stumbled into the side wall, rocks scraping along her skin. "Come on, woman. Survival first. Love life later."

She felt her way along a passage that was getting more confined with every step. The walls were closing in on her. Literally. And she had nowhere else to go. She couldn't climb back up the shaft with a possibly broken arm, let alone reach the opening she'd come through. There had to be another way. "Please! Can anyone hear me?"

"I hear you," a voice said from the dark.

Goose pimples budded along the back of her neck. Not just any voice. His voice. She'd been right about the rash on Becker's wrist, about the one on her neck. They hadn't come from a peanut allergy, but asbestos. The killer had been in this mine. Just like all the men and women who'd walked away sick. She backed into the wall, trying to make herself as small as possible. Clicking off the flashlight, she cast herself into darkness in hopes he couldn't see her, but the sensation of being watched refused to let up. "You."

"Yes, Avalynn. Me." The voice that'd lodged into her mind all those years ago surrounded her, bumping off the walls and attacking her from every angle. It elicited a guttural reaction that shoved acid into her throat. "I was hoping to see you again, but I have to admit, this is the last place I expected to find you."

She licked at her dry, dust-caked lips. Her voice cracked. "Penny... Where is she?"

"Ah. And here I thought you'd come to pay me a visit." The direction of his voice changed. How? Where was he hiding? He was playing games with her—she knew that—but the effect triggered a kaleidoscope of insignificance and doubt. "After all, we're old friends, aren't we?"

Shuffling registered from her right, and she moved farther along the wall, away from it. A kick of dirt seemed to hitch right in front of her. Macie crouched, clutching the flashlight with everything she had. She was ready. To end this. To leave the past behind. To have a life outside of trauma and fear and loneliness. "Friends? Is that what you'd call this? You tried to kill me. You killed Hazel and Sakari. Now you have Penny. I'm sorry to be the one to tell you, but this friendship is really one-sided."

"Oh, that's not the way I see it, Macie," he said.

Her instincts picked up on the use of her current name. Something he hadn't done until now. It was... almost familiar. Friendly. Terrifying.

"I mean, you talked to me every day, never knowing I was the one who found you in those woods with little Hazel all those years ago." He was moving again, trying to confuse her. "You smiled at me. Laughed with me. You trusted me with your deepest frustrations at work and recommended the books you'd read. Puppetry, how humankind relates to and reacts to plants—all kinds of subjects I never would've considered without your interest. That's what I love about you. Your curiosity. I like to think that makes us similar in that respect. You see, I'm very creative as well. Not in the same way as you, but Hazel and Sakari certainly appreciated my art."

An outline solidified a few feet away, then moved away, and realization struck. He didn't know where she was. He was trying to keep her talking to get her location. Just as she was doing to him. "There I go again. Talking on and on about myself, and you listening so intently. If that's not friendship, what is?"

Horror churned in her gut. No. It wasn't possible. She would've known. She would've known the second he'd spoken to her that first time. She would've recognized him for what he truly was. Wouldn't she? Macie ran through the massive catalog of people she interacted with on a daily basis. There were just too many faces. She'd recommended thousands of books over the past six years and had complained to most people in this town about her job as a dispatcher. It was how she'd gotten so many of them to stay on the line until help arrived.

The man in the dark could be anyone.

"I feel you need a moment," he said. "And I agree, it's a lot to take in. I'm sure it's not every day you realize you brought this—all of this—on yourself."

A flashlight lit up in the too small space and blinded her. Macie brought her uninjured hand up to block the light, but it was too late. He'd found her. She launched off the ground and ran for the way she'd come.

Pain spiraled across her back as a collision of muscle tackled her. The wall rushed to meet her face, and she was suddenly pinned between her attacker and the mineshaft that'd nearly killed her. Strong hands flipped her around to face him, but still, the beam of the flashlight blocked his features.

He swept his thumb above her upper lip, coming away with blood seeping into dry, cracked fingers between them. "Well, now, look what you made me do." Real disappointment dipped his voice into dangerous territory. "I'll have to adjust my plans accordingly. No bother. I like the challenge."

"I don't know what you're so upset about." Macie tried to ignore the deep ache exploding across her face. It was a small price to pay to turn her into a victim. Because that was the only way he wouldn't consider her a threat. He couldn't divide his attention between her and Penny. If she wasn't a threat, he might take her to wherever Penny was being held. It was a solid plan. Riggs might've been proud. If he was here. "I'm the one who's bleeding."

"Bleeding or not, I'm going to enjoy this." He dragged her away from the wall, and Macie released her flashlight.

As much as she wanted to use it as a weapon, she needed to get to Penny. These tunnels went on for miles and in every which direction. The deeper she searched, the faster she'd get herself lost or killed. But he'd have a map. Either mentally or physically, he could work his way back to his captive. She let him shove her ahead of him, his beam only lighting up a couple steps ahead. "Glad one of us is."

"You're awfully chipper for someone about to die." Another hint of familiarity brushed against her mind.

Macie almost wanted to laugh. She wasn't going to die. At least not until she got Penny out of this literal hellhole. By then, maybe Riggs would realize she hadn't stayed put at the cabin. Her heart thudded harder at the mere thought of his name. And with that one thought came an array of memories, starting from when she'd first set eyes on him more than twenty-five years ago to him showing up on her doorstep and beyond. Staring down at her with the sheets tucked over their heads, their hands interlaced together after they survived the attack in the woods, to his cringe when he took a bite of Jolly Rancher breakfast pastries at the kitchen table.

He'd turned his back on her, thought of her as nothing more than a coward, but she wanted him. Warts and all. His constant alertness, his difficulty in trusting people, the isolation he insisted on carrying with him everywhere he went—all of it had molded him into the man she'd started falling in love with as a ten-year-old. The one she'd probably always loved. "Whether I die or not isn't going to change anything. You'll keep looking to scratch that itch that compels you to terrorize and kill little girls, and the rest of the world will keep turning. But in the end, I'll know I did everything in my power to stop you. Just like Detective Becker did."

A hard shove thrust her forward, and Macie hit the dirt. Her arm bellowed for relief. She rolled onto her back, ready for the next strike, but it never came.

"Well, you saw how that worked out for him." The killer moved into the light, exposing an all-too-familiar face. He was right. She had considered him a friend. All these years, she'd been blind, coming to him for advice and shared jokes. How hadn't she seen it? "Let's see how that works out for you."

"ISLA'S NOT ABLE to get an exact location." Alma Majors brought up a local map on her phone and set it between the three of them on the dusty kitchen table. "Wherever Macie is, it's too remote. The best she can do is give us the truck's last position it pinged."

Riggs didn't know the area. He had no idea where to look for Macie, but a last position was better than nothing. He pointed to the small blue dot superimposed over the map with pale brown background. "This looks like mountain terrain. Where exactly is this?"

"It's a one-way road heading up the mountain. Only problem is that single road meets up with Cinnamon Pass." Majors expanded the view on her phone. "From there, she could be anywhere west of the range. Ouray, Ironton, Ridgway—those are just a few of the towns on the other side. She didn't say anything about where she was headed?"

"No. We… I left her here. Alone." And it'd been the biggest mistake of his life. Right up there with turning his back on Becker last year. He'd given her his word he would protect her, yet he'd done to her just as she'd done to Hazel all those years ago. That didn't make him any better. Hell, it made this whole thing worse. The photo he'd discarded at his feet pulled his attention from the phone. Seconds were ticking by—too fast. Penny's countdown had reached under twelve hours. Whatever they were going to do, they needed to do it now. "This photo was on the top of the pile on the floor when we got here, but I know for a fact it was closer to the bottom when I left. Macie dragged it out. She saw something. Something that convinced her leaving was the best option."

"That looks like an allergic reaction." It was Majors's turn with the last photo taken of his partner. This was all he'd have when this case was closed. Just photos. He only hoped the next autopsies weren't of Macie and Penny. The thought sickened him.

"You think the killer had something on his hands that transferred to them?" Gregson studied the pat-

tern across Becker's wrist. "Macie's allergic to peanuts. She threatens to curse me every time I bring
trail mix into the break room. What are the chances
your partner had the same allergy and the killer happened to have traces days apart still on his hands?"

"You're right. It doesn't make sense. Even if he
hadn't washed his hands, he was in those woods, he
handled Penny and fought me. It would've wiped
off." Riggs was studying the photo upside down now.
In a different perspective, he could make out the
angry edges of each blister. Like a burn. He took the
photo from Majors and flipped it around. "I don't
think this is a food allergy."

"Chemical." Majors glanced at her partner, her
features softening. "Chief Ford pulled a body out
of a refrigerator over a year ago, before any of us
got here. One that'd been buried underground. A
young woman the killer had to get rid of before she
informed Dr. Miles she was in danger."

He straightened. Macie hadn't told him any of
that. How many homicides had this town seen lately?

Gregson maneuvered around the table to close the
distance between him and his partner, almost like
he didn't even know he was doing it.

Majors collected her phone from the table and
tapped the screen. Once. Twice. "I've seen the case
file and the autopsy photos. The victim suffocated
inside that refrigerator. There were signs of a struggle all over her body, but she also had burns like this

on her hands and the side of her face. Like she'd laid down in something." She handed the phone over, leaning back into Gregson's support. "Dr. Miles wasn't able to match the reaction to anything at the time. Her operation is pretty small at the funeral home, and everything has to go through the state crime lab, but it's been long enough. She might have the results."

He skimmed through the case file. Everything Majors had said lined up with the report. Female victim, died of suffocation due to lack of oxygen in the refrigerator. Bruising, lacerations and a rash-like reaction had all been noted in the report. All bodily fluids, bone, organ, muscle and skin samples had been sent to Unified Crime Lab in Denver. Nothing to notate of any updates or what had caused the reaction. "Call Dr. Miles. I want to know if she's received the results back from the crime lab on the samples she sent."

"You got it, boss." Gregson slid his hand over his partner's stomach and whispered something in her ear before he headed for the door, phone in hand.

Riggs didn't have the courage to take in the full interaction. Not without his heart squeezing so tight he couldn't breathe. Less than twenty-four hours ago, he'd had that. That connection with another person. That one-of-a-kind, hurl yourself off a cliff determination to throw your life away and forget everything you believed in optimism. Because of Macie. He couldn't deny that he'd thought about what might've happened between them if he hadn't left her here on her own. He certainly wouldn't be searching for her now—that was for damn sure. Riggs swept the rest of the files off the floor and stacked them in random order. He'd have to go through them all over again to straighten them out. "You're pregnant."

Majors hitched her thumbs in her service belt. "You're good. No one else has said anything. Or maybe they're too scared to say anything to me. Not sure which."

"You know what you're having?" Riggs was suddenly invested in the answer. As though it mattered. Any of it. Macie was out there. Possibly fighting for her life, for Penny's, and he wanted to know about the intricacies of two officers—partners—starting a family and their lives together.

"Too soon to tell." She shook her head. "Cree doesn't let me out of his sight. He tried to convince the chief to take me off duty, but I shut that down the second I found out. I've wasted too much time being scared. I gave up an entire career because of it. Moved to a town I didn't know where I was isolated and alone before getting my head on straight. I let it rule over every decision I made. I'm done with that. I want to live every moment of the life I have left. On my terms and with the people I love."

Love. The word battered through Riggs's brain until it was all he could think about. He'd been in love before. He'd married, had plans for the future, and when that future hadn't played out, he'd committed himself to the work to try to make up for it. And when the job hadn't fulfilled him, he'd taken a hard look at where his life had derailed, blaming it all on Becker. But with Macie... That word felt different. Real. He'd spent years trying to come to terms with losing Macie and Hazel all in the same week. He'd hitched his life to Becker's, joined the academy, worked his way up the ladder into detective and homicide—none of it had made him feel the way she had in three short days.

"The cases we work, the victims we seek justice for," Majors said. "It takes a toll, doesn't it? Sometimes we forget what's important and who we are. We become the work to the point it's consumed our lives, but take it from me, Riggs, it will never be enough."

She was right. He needed Macie back. Needed to make things right. Because he loved her. The good, the questionable, the obsessive—all of her. A piece of him had been missing the day she'd extracted herself from his life, and he'd only had a taste of what that wholeness had felt like when he'd come to Battle Mountain. He couldn't give it up again. "How did you stop?"

Majors glanced toward the door her partner had exited, that permanent hitch to her mouth deepening. "I realized I didn't have to save the world alone.

I could make more of a difference with a partner who had my back in a small town who needs my help more than ever."

Riggs didn't have an answer for that.

Gregson shoved through the front door, fighting back a rush of dirt and wind. "Dr. Miles is sending over the lab results. We should have them in a couple minutes." The former ATF agent took his expected position at his partner's side. "You good?"

"Never better." Majors smiled, and Gregson's face dissolved from duty to outright adoration. His feelings for the woman showed in perfect balance. Not all or nothing, and Riggs couldn't look away from the easiness of it all. These officers trusted one another, would put themselves in harm's way for each other—all the while starting their own lives away from the department.

Gregson's phone pinged with an incoming email. "That should be the lab results." The reserve officer swiped his index finger across the screen, his hard gaze narrowing. "That doesn't make sense."

"What is it?" Riggs rounded the table, trying to get a better look at the screen.

"This says the rash found on the victim's face and hands from the refrigerator was caused by a direct contact reaction to asbestos," Gregson said. "But she was found in a mine."

"A mine?" Hell, there had to be dozens of them in Battle Mountain. The town had been built from the profits and economy of big mining. They weren't any closer to an answer than when they'd started, and the killer wasn't just going to wait for them to catch up. They had to do something now.

"The road Isla's truck's GPS pinged." Majors set her phone back on the table and widened the map view on the screen. "It meets up with Cinnamon Pass, but there's a branch that passes the last mine to be shut down. It's the same one where the chief found that first victim."

"Which one?" He was ready. Not just to fight for Penny and Macie but for their future. And nothing was going to get in his way this time. Especially not himself.

"It's not safe, Riggs." Majors shook her head. "The government shut it down for a reason. None of us know the conditions or if we'll even be able to breathe in there."

He didn't care. He'd already lost everything. Now was his time to step up and take it back. "Which mine, Majors?"

She glanced at her partner, who nodded, then back to Riggs. "Desolation."

Chapter Fourteen

The dark was playing tricks on her mind. She was hallucinating the face of the man who'd hidden in the shadows. Or maybe it was her brain mixing up signals. Right? That was the only explanation.

"You…" Macie shoved her heels into the ground, hoping to gain some distance between her and her captor, but she couldn't leave. She couldn't abandon Penny the way she'd abandoned Hazel all those years ago. "How?"

"Uncomfortable, isn't it?" Reagan Allen stood over her, offering his hand to help her up. The lines in his face had deepened since she'd seen him three days ago, his nose a bit more crooked. The strike she'd delivered during their altercation in the woods must have broken it, turning him almost unrecognizable. Such a small difference, but one that changed everything. "Seeing someone for who they really are."

It was all coming back to her now. The flashes of memory she'd tried to bury. His hair was the same color, if speckled with a few silver strands at the temples. He had a beard now, too. Better to hide his face. All this time, she'd convinced herself she would see him coming, that she would know his voice, but the preparation, the fear, the drive she held on to get her through—it'd all been for nothing. He'd been right in front of her this entire time. "You've been hiding in Battle Mountain all these years. You pretended you were a pastry chef and a coffee shop owner and joked with everyone who came into Caffeine and Carbs. Why?"

"I wasn't pretending. I'm a very good pastry chef. I didn't lie about that, and I didn't lie about my background. The pastry world got the best of me. The pressure to compete and become the best after years of study and burns and thousands of hours of pushing myself to the top… I'll be honest. I snapped." Reagan retracted his bandaged hand when she refused to take it. "I found myself in the middle of the woods, walking aimlessly, until I heard two little girls laughing. They were throwing chunks of moss at each other, like nothing in the world could take away their joy. I wanted that. What they had. So I took it."

She couldn't breathe, couldn't think. All of this—the lives stolen, the years living in fear alone and as someone else—had all started because a pastry chef couldn't handle the pressures of his career? She had to suppress the desire to laugh. No, something in him snapped long before that. He'd just needed an excuse to go over the edge entirely.

Reagan latched his hand around her arm and hauled Macie to her feet like she was nothing more than a rag doll. "But to answer your question, killing people requires income, Avalynn. Strategy. Equipment. I had to hold a day job and make myself part of the community. Here, in this pathetic, going nowhere town, I could still do what I did best. Bake. But when that pressure starts getting to me again…"

"You kidnap and murder innocent girls." That was why she and Riggs hadn't been able to discern a pattern between Hazel's, Sakari's and Penny's abductions. This wasn't compulsion. This was pleasure. A reward for a job well-done.

"You of all people should understand. When the pressure gets to be too much for your job with the department, where do you come?" He didn't wait for an answer, maneuvering her along the tunnel, deeper into the mountain. "My misuse of violence is the same as your misuse of caffeine, Avalynn. They might be different mediums, but we both get what we want in the end. Release."

She tried to memorize every step, to make sure she and Penny took the right way out, but there were too many turns. Too many ways to get lost. "Strangling people and drinking too much coffee aren't the same. I don't hurt anyone."

"True, but to each our own." Reagan led her into a

larger cavern. The walls gleamed with metallic flecks that would turn any miner's head. Braces held up the ceiling, angling out to take the weight of the earth above, but she'd read enough stories to know one shift in the rock, one more pound of pressure, could bring it all crumbling down on top of them.

A whimper echoed off the cavern.

Macie ripped her arm out of Reagan's grip. Her heart shot into her throat. She took two more steps inside, searching every corner and shadow. "Penny, is that you?"

"Macie?" The little girl moved into the flashlight beam. The sound of chains rubbing against each other stopped as the fetters pulled tight when Penny tried to run for her.

Macie took another step to meet her but was wrenched back against the killer's chest.

"Ah, ah, ah. I believe that's far enough." He set his mouth against her ear, triggering a rush of disgust and shivers. "I've seen what the two of you can do when you work together. If you don't mind my caution, I'd prefer you to sit over here." He hauled her to the opposite side of the cavern and forced Macie to sit. "Mind the patch of asbestos." He waved his bandaged hand in front of her. "It's a real buzzkill."

Rock bit into the backs of her thighs and aggravated the soreness from her fall. She stared up into the face of a man she'd trusted with pieces of herself. All this time, he'd just been using them against her.

But she'd found Penny. The four-year-old chained a few feet away was the one and only goal. In the end, Macie recalled the turns they'd taken from that original tunnel she'd fallen into. She might not be able to make it back up the shaft to the surface, but Penny could. She just had to get her there.

"Now, don't you worry, Avalynn. There's plenty of time for you and I to get reacquainted with each other. After all, you're going to be here awhile." He turned his back to her, closing in on his younger victim. "Penny, on the other hand—her time is up."

Not as long as Macie could help it. She felt along the wall he'd set her against. It wasn't uncommon for miners to leave tools behind after their shifts, but she couldn't find anything. The killer had ensured nothing could be used as a weapon against him. Except the very earth holding them captive. She ran her hand behind her. Penny's soft cry grew louder now. Macie clutched a section of the wall jutting out, filling her palm with its size. It broke away in her hand, and she clutched it with everything she had left. "Not yet."

Macie shoved to her feet, swinging the rock as hard as she could. The makeshift weapon connected with Reagan's skull. He dropped to his knees, then face-first onto the ground. She didn't have time for victory. She needed every second he was unconscious to get Penny out of the chains and back into the tunnels. After tossing the rock, she collected the killer's flashlight, then darted for the girl. The shackle had been bolted into what looked like a long stretch of railroad steel. There was no way Penny could move in these tunnels with a ton of metal dragging behind her. Macie tested the strength of the anklet. It was bolted shut. No key. No tools in sight, but there had to be something Reagan had used to secure her. "It's okay. I'm here."

"Don't leave me, Macie." Penny latched on to Macie's injured arm, digging her fingernails deep into sensitive skin. "I want to go home. I want Mommy."

"I won't leave you. I promise." Macie ran dirty fingers through the girl's hair. "We have to hurry. Did you see where he put the tool to tighten this?"

Penny pointed past Macie's shoulder. "It's in his pocket."

She turned back. Reagan's outline hadn't moved. He was still unconscious from the look of it, but that could change at any moment. Shifting his weight might even trigger his brain to reboot, but she had to risk it. There wasn't anything else in this cavern that would get Penny free from the cuff. "Stay back."

Macie got to her feet, before approaching Reagan as quietly as an echoing chamber of emptiness allowed. Her stomach rumbled, and she closed her eyes, wishing it to stay quiet. Only her breathing registered. She stilled near his head, then slowly worked her way around to his midsection. He was wearing a coat. Any one of the pockets could hold the tool she needed, but her instincts said he'd used one of his pants pockets so it'd always stay with him. Her exhale sounded too loud in her ears, and she waited to see if it brought Reagan around.

Nothing.

She could do this. For Penny. For all the other little girls who would be caught in the bastard's web if she didn't. Macie bent down, pressing one hand into Reagan's shoulder, and shook him gently. No response. With a last glance toward Penny, she felt her way through his back pockets, then the ones in his jacket that hadn't been pinned between him and raw earth. The tool wasn't there. She took a deep breath.

Then rolled Reagan onto his back.

His head flopped to one side, away from her in the shadow. Macie felt along his front pockets. There. The length of a wrench peeked out from the right side. She slid it free as quickly as she dared. Her heart threatened to beat straight out of her chest. Too hard. Too fast. Steel warmed in her hand as she backed away. She couldn't believe Reagan was still unconscious.

Macie fit the end of the wrench against the bolt keeping Penny hostage and twisted until it started unscrewing. "Almost there."

The bolt hit the ground. Penny was free. She grabbed the flashlight and hauled the girl into her arms. Her injured arm screamed with every movement, but she had to push through. They rushed for the entrance Reagan had brought Macie through. She'd taken a left in. She went right this time. The number of steps had gotten lost sometime in the mix of pain and surprise, but this section of the tunnel looked familiar.

Penny's arms tightened around her neck, keeping her grounded and in the moment. It'd be easy to panic, to succumb to the fear they'd never make it out of this maze alive, but Macie had lived afraid long enough. It was time to start taking action. No more false identities. No more lies or distance from the people she so desperately wanted in her life—people like Penny and Weston and Campbell, even Easton. No more running. Battle Mountain was her home, and she was sure as hell going to fight for a life here.

The tunnel came to an abrupt end. Macie pulled up short, one hand secured at the back of Penny's head. She dropped the flashlight, giving them just enough light. "We're here, but you're going to have to climb up this shaft. See?" Macie pointed straight up, to the hole in the ceiling. "This will take you right to the surface. I want you to run as fast as you can to the entrance of the mine and down the road. Understand?"

"You can't climb that. Your arm hurts." The four-year-old had more awareness than anyone gave her credit for.

"You're right. I can't. I have to find another way out." Tears burned in Macie's eyes. The chances of finding another way out, without running into Reagan to finish the job, were slim. But that was the cost of loving someone, wasn't it? Risking it all. "But you can bet your little behind I'm going to get out of here. Okay?"

"Promise?" Penny asked.

"Promise." Macie offered her little finger and made it official. "Okay. Up you go, squirt." It took three tries to maneuver Penny onto her shoulder to lift her toward the shaft, but from the stories Kendric and Campbell told, the troublemaker had gotten herself into far more precarious situations than this. "Use your feet and grab on to anything you can. You can do it."

Penny tested the climb out for herself, managing to make it a couple feet.

"Great work. Keep going." The tears were streaking into her hairline now. It didn't look like it, but this was goodbye. "I'll be seeing you soon. Okay?"

"Okay." Penny leveraged her feet against the rock wall and moved up another couple of feet. Faster than Macie expected, she was gone.

Pain exploded across her face as a fist connected with her cheek. She hit the ground. White spots flittered across her vision, blocking out the threat.

Reagan's voice surrounded her a split second before a hand latched around her neck. "I'm so very disappointed in you, Avalynn, and I'm tired of this game."

Riggs studied the footprints cast into the dirt leading straight into the mouth of darkness. Too many to get any idea of who'd come and gone. For an abandoned mine, Desolation seemed like the place to be.

Wind rustled through thick pines on either side of the short incline leading up to the entrance. A low whistle reached his ears from inside, almost like a warning. "Light it up."

Both Majors and Gregson powered their flashlights and took a position at his rear. They were headed into an unknowable situation, with an unknowable killer and an unknowable amount of danger. Mines weren't closed or abandoned on a whim. The three of them crossed the threshold into pitch-blackness as one.

Riggs watched his every step. Thick supports braced up along either wall and crossed the ceiling above him in expertly measured intervals. The familiar scent of gravel and humidity dived into his lungs as he searched along the tunnel. His footsteps echoed off the walls the deeper he walked into the mountain. The beam from his flashlight landed on a mound of dirt up ahead. Like someone had dug a hole. In reality, someone had. Weston Ford and Dr. Chloe Miles had dragged a body out of a refrigerator in that hole less than two years ago.

Seemed where this town's history with violence had started, Riggs had the privilege and duty to see it through to the end. "Keep an ear out. Anything out of the ordinary, you send out the warning."

"What's out of the ordinary for a mine that hasn't

been operational for six years?" Gregson grunted after a hard thud. His partner had sucker punched him. "Hey, I think it's a valid question."

A pattering reached his ears, and Riggs pulled up short. His instincts homed in on the sound, trying to differentiate it from familiar noises. "Hear that?"

The same rhythm thumped hard from the inky darkness.

And it was growing louder.

"Footsteps," Majors said. "One set. Coming fast."

Riggs unholstered his weapon. Whoever it was, they wouldn't be expecting three armed officers. Since the first time he'd joined this investigation, he and his backup held the advantage here.

"Police!" Gregson's voice rang too loud in Riggs's ears. "Slow down and approach with your hands behind your head."

The footsteps didn't falter.

Tension tightened the tendons along Riggs's neck and shoulders. Those footsteps. They weren't normal. Weren't heavy. Understanding hit. "Put down your weapons." Riggs broke his position and rushed forward, causing both Gregson and Majors to lower their aim. "Penny?"

A quiet sob joined the rush of footsteps as the girl broke through the shadows. Riggs dropped to his knees, arms out to catch her. She collided with his chest, nearly knocking him off-balance. "It's okay.

You're safe, Penny. You're safe." He tried to pry her small face from his shoulder. "Where is Macie?"

"She couldn't climb up with me. Her arm was hurt. She said to run as fast as I could." Penny wiped grimy fingers across her face. "I did what she said. Can I go home now? Can I please go home?"

Couldn't climb? His brain worked to translate a four-year-old's perspective. Climbing could mean a shaft. If Macie had fallen, she could be hurt. Not to mention she was still being hunted by a killer. "Penny, where did you climb from?"

"Back there in the tunnel." The girl pointed behind her. Into the unknown. "She pushed me up inside, and I climbed all the way up. Just like she told me. Before the bad man got us."

"The bad man's here?" He felt more than saw her nod. That was all the information he needed. Riggs handed Penny over to Majors, who instantly secured her arms around the girl. He had no doubt the duo who'd had his back would do whatever it took to keep Penny safe. "Radio her parents. Tell them where we are, and make sure you get her home to them."

Gregson stepped forward. "You can't go in there alone, man. This place is a maze. You'll never make it out."

"Albuquerque caves aren't too different from Battle Mountain mines, and I've investigated plenty of them." Riggs removed his jacket and rolled up his sleeves. The less he had to carry, the better. Never knew when the walls would start closing in. "Just make sure she gets home."

"At least take one of our radios and an extra flashlight. We'll send another unit your way as soon as we can." Gregson stretched out his hand. "Good luck."

Riggs shook, feeling that spark of partnership and community for the first time in years. He'd had that once. With Becker. Hell, he wasn't sure he'd ever feel it again. He accepted the extra equipment. "Thanks."

He didn't wait to watch them take Penny back to the patrol car. Every second Macie was down here was another second she might not make it out alive, and he just couldn't live with that outcome. Not after everything it'd taken for him to get her back in his life. He was here for her, and he wasn't going anywhere until she was back in his arms.

The mine seemed to breathe around him, fluctuations in smells and some kind of breeze changing with every step. Places like this had to have airflow to avoid gasses getting trapped in certain rooms where miners had been working, but the possibility of death at every turn kept his nerves at a high point. It was worth it. Every risk, every potential for a life-ending step. For Macie.

The ground sloped downward, taking him deeper into the belly of the beast. He wasn't sure how far he'd gone or if he was even walking in a straight line anymore. The walls were more narrow here, funneling him into unfamiliar territory. Rocks reached out and grabbed for his gun, his extra flashlight, his shirt. They were everywhere, but none of it detracted from that feeling of being watched. The same feeling he'd experienced in the woods before losing Penny a second time.

"I'll give you until the count of three to release her and come out with your hands behind your back." His words echoed back to him.

"Detective Karig, I knew we'd meet again." It was the same voice. The one that'd haunted Riggs's nightmares for the past two days. "Unfortunately, Macie is unavailable at the moment. Perhaps I can take a message. Let her know you'd stopped by when she's conscious. You see, she took somewhat of a nasty fall. She's going to need to save her energy. You understand."

Riggs halted his approach. As much as he wanted to believe his senses, he couldn't trust them in a place like this. He'd learned that the hard way when he'd gotten stabbed in the thigh. Clutching his flashlight, he hit the power button and cast himself into darkness. Relying only on what he could see would waste time. Time Macie didn't have. "You're trapped in here, you son of a bitch. BMPD has the place surrounded. Every exit. There's no way out for you, and the more time you stall, the worse it's going to be. Why not save yourself the trouble?"

"Where's the fun in that?" the killer asked.

The air shifted, and Riggs took a step back a

split second before a blade slashed across his face. He grabbed for where he believed the killer's upper body to be and clenched both hands into the bastard's shoulders. Riggs thrust his head forward and connected with flesh and bone. His shoulder screamed at the impact, but he only pushed himself harder.

The killer cried out.

Riggs threw a right hook and landed a hard blow. The blade whined again. He caught the killer's wrist and tucked his shoulder beneath the man's rib cage. Hauling him overhead, Riggs slammed Penny's abductor to the ground. He fought to take a whole breath. "You are under arrest for the abduction of Penny Dwyer, for the abduction of Macie Barclay, wanted in the questioning of Sakari Vigil's murder, wanted for questioning of Hazel McAdams's murder, for killing my partner, Kevin Becker, and whatever the hell else I can pin on you."

He unholstered his cuffs and dragged the killer into the flashlight beam. Disbelief crushed air from his lungs, and his grip faltered. The baker from the coffee shop? All this time, he'd been watching Macie, getting her to trust him. Riggs ratcheted the cuffs into place. "The building Becker was found strangled. It was your building, the one that burned. You lured him there, didn't you? Right before you killed him. Why?"

"You know, I couldn't believe it when he walked right into my bakery asking if I knew of anyone named Macie Barclay. He told me everything," Reagan said. "How he believed she was part of a murder investigation from twenty-five years ago in Albuquerque. That he needed to find her to ask her about the day her best friend had been abducted and murdered. You see, Avalynn made a mistake. She's been investigating Hazel's case all this time, relying on others to get her the information she needed. Seemed one of them spilled the beans to Becker, and he came running. But I wasn't going to let him take her from me."

Riggs tightened the cuffs more than needed. "She's not yours, you son of a bitch."

"She's not yours either, Detective. Did you really think after staying under the radar for twenty-five years, this would be easy? You arrest me, Avalynn dies." Reagan Allen heaved to catch his breath. Blood leaked from a gash on his head, bruising darkening his nose and cheekbones. Nothing like the man who'd given him a donut a few days ago. "You're going to have to make a choice. Take me into the station or keep Avalynn from dying a horrible, painful death. You couldn't save your partner. Are you going to save the woman you love?"

Riggs shoved the bastard against the opposite wall. "Where is she?"

"I'll give you a clue as soon as you get me out of these cuffs," he said.

Variables raced through his mind. Arrest Reagan

and save dozens—if not hundreds—of more girls just like Penny and Hazel, or save the one woman he couldn't see himself live without.

"I'll take it from here." Another flashlight brightened in Riggs's peripheral vision, blocking out the man behind the beam. A ten-gallon hat took shape in the shadows as he sauntered closer with all the time in the world. "Seems Mr. Allen and I sure have a lot to talk about anyway."

Riggs raised one hand to protect his retinas. "Who the hell are you?"

"I'm the chief of this town, Detective." A man, similar in stature and features as Easton Ford, stepped into the light. Maybe a few years younger. A day's worth of beard growth intensified the sharp angles of his oval face and brought out the seriousness in his eyes. The rightful chief lowered his flashlight with one hand and aimed his sidearm at Reagan Allen with the other. "You've done good. Now, I'm going to need you to bring my dispatcher home. My entire department is falling apart without her. Take the radio. I've got this covered."

"Yes, sir." A renewed energy lit him up from the inside, but without Reagan's clue as to where he'd set up Macie, he was looking for a needle in a five-mile deep mine haystack. Horrible, painful death. That was what Reagan had said. The killer's MO had stuck with strangulation thus far. All past victims had suffocated. He wanted the control, to make them suffer and lead them through a slow death.

Riggs didn't believe the bastard would change at the end. He'd have her somewhere that was possible. In a mine, that could mean a small room with low oxygen or a contraption that applied pressure. His instincts said the former was the easiest to set up quickly. He just had to find her in time. "Macie!"

Chapter Fifteen

Her name spliced through the comforting warmth she'd buried herself inside. *Macie!*

Heavy. Everywhere. Her fingers had gone numb. She couldn't feel her feet. Something was strapped over her nose and mouth. The forced air froze her nostrils and throat. But the pain in her arm had settled to a dull ache. How was that possible?

"You got your wish, Detective," a female voice said. "She's coming around. I'll give you two a minute."

Macie willed her eyes to open. Dim lighting infiltrated her cracked lids. There were no lights in the mine, but she'd had a flashlight. A dark outline blocked the assault, and every muscle she owned tightened with battle-ready tension. Reagan. She gripped something cold and solid, ready to fight back with everything she had left. No matter how weak she felt.

"Macie, it's me," he said.

She knew that voice, but this had to be some kind

of dream. Her brain synapses were probably firing all kinds of information in the last minutes of her life. Riggs wasn't here. Reagan had won. He'd finally claimed her in the end.

A calloused hand smoothed over hers. So real. "You were down in the mine. You fought back, and we arrested Reagan Allen. You're in the hospital now. You did it, Macie. You brought him down. You found Hazel's killer."

Was this…real? She wouldn't make that up, would she? The feel of his hand in hers felt solid. If this wasn't real, she sucked at coming up with ideas of heaven, that was for sure. This place was worse than the cabin in the desert. Macie tested her hold on him, and a sob broke free. "Am I dead?"

"No, Red. You're very much not dead," he said.

"It's over?" She'd spent years trying to find the man who'd killed her best friend, but there was only one small soul she cared about right then. Her throat convulsed around the dryness. The memories were there. No sense in burying them this time. It wouldn't make the pain go away. Just as trying to forget what she'd done to Hazel hadn't destroyed her grief. Macie tried to bring her hand to her face. Her fingers collided with a rubbery mask. An oxygen mask. "Penny. Where's—"

"She's home." Riggs's face cleared with every inhale. So stupidly handsome. This was real. He was here. He threaded his hand in her hair, and her skin goose bumped at his touch. "She's got a couple scrapes and bruises, but she's been checked out. She had very little exposure to the asbestos, it turns out, and she should live a long and happy life. Because of you."

Penny was safe. The weightlessness of that truth took the oxygen straight out of her lungs. She closed her eyes as the past slipped from her grip and a bright future took hold. It was over. She was free. Reagan Allen would pay for what he'd done to those girls, and she could finally choose a life on her terms. "What happened?"

"Reagan trapped you in one of the small ventless caverns. The gasses from the mine were pretty strong. Doctors weren't sure you'd ever wake up with oxygen levels as low as yours." Anguish shook his voice, and Riggs tightened his hold in her hair. "I don't know how long you were in there, but you were close to dead when I found you. It's a miracle you're still here. I don't know what I would've done if I hadn't gotten to you in time. You've been out of it for about three days. I thought I might have to go beat the living daylights out of Reagan if you didn't wake up."

"What do you mean?" Her heart rate picked up the pace. She didn't dare hope. Not yet. Because hope led to disappointment and hurt, and she didn't want to go through that again. He'd accused her of only looking out for herself. Said that she hadn't changed from that selfish ten-year-old he'd known.

"I mean I was wrong." He tested a cut across her temple, so gentle and warm. Riggs wasn't looking at her, not directly. "About everything. About this case, about you. I found the files, Macie. In your duffel bag. You never said anything. You've been looking for Reagan Allen all this time."

What was there to say? Of course, she had. "It was my fault Hazel died. I was just trying to—"

"To make it right." That unreadable gaze was on her then, and the world threatened to tip on its axis. He had that power—the one that changed her perception and made her forget anything else existed. He could turn her world upside down in the blink of an eye, and she wouldn't even mind. Because she trusted he would put it right back where it belonged. Riggs interlaced his fingers with hers and traced her busted knuckles with his thumb. "You risked your life all these years trying to identify the man in the woods, knowing what would happen if you did so. You left your family, ended friendships, went on the run. You sacrificed an entire life to bring him down. You knew any steps you took could alert Reagan to what you were doing, and you did it anyway."

She didn't know what to say to that.

"And I was wrong, Macie." He kissed the back of her hand, triggering a whirlwind of butterflies in her stomach. "You're not the same girl I knew back then. Not even a little bit. You're so much more. You're brave, and selfless, and loving. You're everything I want in my life and everything I've been pushing away, and I love you, damn it. I always have. And I'm sorry I wasted what little time we've had trying to prove I don't need you. Because I do. All of you."

She wanted to believe him. She wanted every word out of his mouth to be true. Macie swallowed around the ache in her throat. The mask was making it hard to breathe, despite the steady flow of oxygen, and she moved to pull it down. "You broke my heart, Riggs. You told me you didn't want me in your life—just as you told Becker you didn't want him in yours anymore—and then you left me in that cabin to protect myself after everything we'd been through. What's going to stop you from cutting ties the next time? What's going to happen when you realize this isn't what you signed up for?"

He focused on their hands intertwined. "I will have to live with those decisions for the rest of my life, Macie, and believe me, it won't be easy. You know the toll it can take. Your mistakes. You've been living with that, too." Riggs retracted his hand from her hair. "I was so convinced I'd been following Becker's career instead of my own path, I rebelled against everything he ever taught me. I'd relied on him for so long, I didn't know if I could catch his killer. Then I found you."

He brought his attention back to her, and an epic shift stripped him of that invisible armor he'd carried since they'd met. "You showed me the worst parts of myself and the best. You showed me what trust feels like and that it can change your entire life. Without you as my partner, Reagan would still be out there, Penny might be dead and I'd spend the rest of my life agonizing over the one case I couldn't ever solve. I'd die just like Becker. Alone, worked to death and without hope. You gave me purpose. You showed me experiencing life comes with letting people in and believing there is good in them. I came to Battle Mountain broken, Macie. You made me strong enough to fix myself. How on earth am I supposed to walk away from all that? From you?"

Her lungs shuddered on a shaky inhale. The tears were back, but they were different than they'd been over the past few days. He loved her. She was the woman he wanted to be with, and for the first time since she'd left Hazel in those woods, she felt whole. No pieces of her missing. She had everything she needed right here. "You know, if you'd just started with that, you could already be kissing me, Detective."

"You got it, Red." Riggs leaned forward off his chair, pressing his mouth to hers. Heat speared through her as he tested her lips, then penetrated the seam of her mouth.

Fisting his shirt in both hands, she dragged him fully into the bed and laid one on him. "I love you, too."

"That's what I like to hear." His laugh diluted the remaining ache in her chest and limbs. "Careful of the shoulder. I'm still recovering from a stab wound."

"We've worked around it once before, and you're still alive." Her arm hadn't been placed in a sling, but she could still feel the muscle soreness from when she'd hit the mine floor after she'd fallen down the shaft. Whatever the case, they could tend to each other's wounds. Physical, mental, emotional. They had all the time in the world.

"I guess now is as good a time as any to ask." Riggs framed her jaw with one hand. "What were you doing with those teddy bears in your sleeping bag in the woods after you downed all that coffee?"

Macie considered her next words very carefully. As much as she loved Riggs, some stories were best left to be doled out in portions. Not an avalanche. Although it would be fun to see his reaction. "You know that secret you promised me and Hazel to never tell? The one where—"

"We made a blood oath, Macie." Shock contorted his handsome face. Riggs straightened, setting one finger over her heart. Right where he'd taken up space. "I still have the scar in my palm to prove it. We promised never to speak of it again."

She raised her hand in the Scout's honor. "And I haven't. I swear, but…" Macie bit her lip, dragging this out as long as possible. It was fun seeing him like this. A combination of the kid he'd been and the man he'd become. It was the start of something new, and she couldn't wait to see what happened next. "The caffeine may have convinced me you and Hazel were the bears."

"You threw a tea party in the middle of the woods with a bunch of stuffed bears." Not a question. But he wasn't running from the room, either.

"It's one of my favorite memories, even if I'm not allowed to talk about it, and I was hopped up on caffeine." She actually didn't remember a whole lot of that night, but she remembered one thing: she'd been happy imagining him and Hazel there. "Do you blame me?"

"I'm never going to be able to unsee that in my head." Riggs locked that molten gaze on her and maneuvered closer. "What did my bear look like?"

"Oh, he was definitely the most handsome. Had the softest hair." She skimmed her fingers through his short hair. "The darkest eyes. And you know what else? He didn't complain about the tea I made."

"Now I know you're making this all up." He leaned back into her, taking her mouth with his, and a flood of laughter caught her by surprise. "But the oath still applies. We're never talking about that tea party again."

HIS TRANSFER WAS OFFICIAL.

The papers had taken a week, and Macie didn't know anything about it yet, but Riggs had no intention of returning to Albuquerque. Not when his life was here in Battle Mountain. From now until she said otherwise, he worked for BMPD.

He hiked the long dirt driveway leading up to Whispering Pines Ranch, his hand in Macie's. She'd hit every milestone her doctor had set for her in the hospital, blowing everyone's expectations out of the water and granting herself an early discharge. She did that. Surprised him at every turn, and he couldn't wait to see where she led them next. He caught a hint of a wheeze as they neared the large main cabin up ahead, and Riggs intentionally stopped to check his bootlaces.

"I know what you're doing," she said.

He couldn't stall anymore. She'd caught him in the act. Riggs straightened, taking her hand in his again. They were late, but he didn't care. The more time he got her to himself before they each went back to work, the better. "I don't know what you're talking about."

"Sure, you don't." She bumped her shoulder into

his as they continued up the too long driveway. "I'm fine. You were there when the doctor said there's going to be some adjustment off the oxygen. The wheezing is normal."

"I could go without the snoring, though." Riggs chanced a glance at her, trying not to smile.

She shoved him away. Shock widened those brilliant green eyes. "I do not snore!"

This was what he loved about them. The easiness, the fluidity between subjects, as if they were reading each other's minds. In truth, he didn't mind the snoring. Just meant she was still in bed with him and not getting wise enough to ditch him for some other guy. Reagan Allen had been arrested and charged for the deaths of Hazel McAdams, Kevin Becker and Sakari Vigil, and it looked like his lawyer was going to get him to plead guilty to avoid the death penalty. The district attorney—Easton Ford's fiancée—would make sure there would be no leniency. The bandage on Reagan's hand had revealed an allergic reaction to asbestos, which sealed the deal of his involvement. Riggs's partner's remains had been released, and without any family to claim Becker, Riggs had taken the old man's burial upon himself. What better place than a small town no one had heard of and where Becker had done one last good deed? "I promise not to tell anyone."

"Thank you." Macie dragged him back to her side

and hooked her arm in his. "After all, I have a reputation to uphold."

Jagged peaks fought to pierce the bright blue sky.
A gaggle of geese called over rocky canyons and
high valley floors. He'd noted a crystalline river
flowing alongside the dirt road they'd taken up here,
promising adventure and spurred endless explora-
tion, before it widened into an impossibly green-blue
lake nestled in a small valley. No matter where he
looked, the possibility captivated him all over again.
Yeah. He could get used to this.

Riggs led her up to the main cabin adorned with
a bright green roof and trim. Smaller satellite cab-
ins had been positioned no more than a few hundred yards in every direction. From what Macie had
told him, Whispering Pines Ranch had started as the
Ford homestead but had since become more bed-
and-breakfast since the death of their old man last
year. Since then, Easton Ford had built a rehabilita-
tion center on the other side of the property. Riggs
could just make out the roof through the trees. This
place… It definitely wasn't a tree house.

"Aunt Macie!" Penny Dwyer practically lunged
down the cabin's steps and raced for Macie's arms.

"Oh, my gosh. Did you somehow get bigger since
the last time I saw you?" Macie hugged the girl tight,
and Riggs's gut clenched as he envisioned what lay
ahead for them. He'd never really thought about a

family given his circumstances and background, but seeing Macie's incredible smile on a bunch of kids would be worth thinking about. "You nearly knocked me over."

"No, I didn't!" Penny laughed.

"You made it." Campbell followed behind her daughter, Kendric positioned at the top of the stairs, watching over his girls. "I was starting to think you'd changed your mind."

"And miss one of Karie's legendary breakfasts? You're out of your mind." Macie let the four-year-old lead her back into the cabin ahead of Riggs, but he was stopped at the top of the stairs.

Kendric Hudson stretched out his hand. "Detective, I just wanted to say thank you. For everything you did to find Penny. I can't imagine where we would be if you and Macie hadn't fought for our daughter. I'm honored to start working with you."

"Same here." Riggs shook, this time without worrying if he was about to die, and nodded to Campbell on the way inside.

Heat closed in on him the moment he stepped over the threshold. A massive stone fireplace climbed two stories up the open main living space. Builder grade wood, lighter than the exterior of the cabin, absorbed the sunlight penetrating through floor-to-ceiling windows on one end of the house. A frayed multicolored crocheted rug took up a majority of

the hardwood floor. A small carved bear holding a
bowl of fruit demanded attention from the table that
stretched the length of the back of the dark leather
sofa, with similar carvings strategically positioned
around the open kitchen and against the grand staircase leading to the second level. Handcrafted lamps,
varying shades of animal fur and muted nature paint-
ings finished the space in old-style hunter decor. This
wasn't just a place for people to live. It was a home.
Something he'd never had.

Macie smiled at him from her position at the
kitchen counter. There were a lot more guests here
than he thought there would be. Easton Ford toasted
a cup of coffee his way with one hand, his other interlaced with a dark-haired woman in a wheelchair
at the head of the massive wood table. From what
he could tell, the older Ford and Genevieve would
have some news of their own to announce soon given
the size of her lower abdomen. A blonde—the coroner—laughed at something Weston Ford said in her
ear while an older woman came to collect the baby
from her arms.

Everyone was smiling, joking, at ease with each
other. Macie seemed right at home, sneaking fresh
fruit from the arrangement on the counter. And he…
didn't know how to do this. The closest thing he'd
had to family was Becker, and he'd screwed that up
to hell and back.

"Don't make direct eye contact. They'll sense your fear." Isla Vachs clenched a cup of coffee, positioning it in front of her mouth as she spoke beside him. The former EMT turned reserve officer tried not to smile at him. And failed. "It's a little overwhelming, isn't it? How invested in each other they all are. You'll get used to it, but if you show any hesitation, they'll throw you in the deep end, make you tell them your whole life story and take personal responsibility to fix it."

"You sound as though you're speaking from experience." Riggs scanned the massive living room. "You're missing the giant you usually have following you around."

"Adan's trying to get a handful of glitter out of his hair for the third time today." Her smile finally gave into a full-blown flash of brilliance. "Mazi believes the world can always use more glitter. In our food, in our bed. Her new idea was in Adan's duffel bag. The whole thing exploded in his face when he opened it."

"Looks like you got hit, too." He pointed at her neck where Isla seemed to sparkle past human capabilities. He had the distinct impression that hadn't been from a duffel bag, though. More like transfer. "I never got to thank you for hiding us out in that dust bowl of yours in the middle of the desert."

"Anything for Macie. Actually, anything for these

guys." Isla hugged her coffee into her chest. "That experience you're talking about. We all have it in spades. There isn't a single one of these people who wouldn't have mine or Adan's or Mazi's backs if we asked, and I wouldn't be here if it weren't for them. I was an outsider. I came out here after I lost everything, and this department welcomed me and Mazi with open arms. They took us in. Made us part of the family."

Riggs didn't understand that. Albuquerque PD had housed nearly nine hundred officers, detectives, administration and specialized department members. Sure, he'd gone out for beers and darts a few times with his fellow teammates, and when the situation called for it, he could trust his brothers and sisters in blue to be at his side. They didn't have brunch together. They didn't hand off their kids to be held by someone else or throw a piece of fruit at another officer's face. He hadn't even done any of that with Becker. Their relationship had been about the work. About saving lives. This... What BMPD had here was more than a department. This was a community. One he wanted to be part of. "That doesn't sound so bad."

"It's not. It's...kind of nice." Isla peeled off to meet Adan coming down the hall, and Riggs worked through the small crowd to join back up with Macie.

"Coffee, Riggs?" Alma Majors lifted a fresh pot

and took a mug from the cabinet, Gregson not far from her side.

"Yes, ma'am, but there's something I gotta do first." Riggs dropped down onto one knee in front of Macie, memorizing every change in her expression. "Macie Barclay, Avalynn Davis, whatever the hell you want to be called, I've wasted enough time trying to go through life on my own." He produced the small gold band with diamonds set in intervals all the way around. "I'm ready to have a partner again. Forever."

The room went quiet, all eyes on them.

Macie's face lit up, and Riggs couldn't get enough of the sight. "You're talking about Adan, aren't you?"

"He's not really my type." Riggs slid one hand beneath hers and pushed the engagement band into place on her finger. "But I'm sure we could work something out, isn't that right, Adan?"

"I told you. We're seeing other people, Karig," Adan said. "It's over."

Laughter filled the room.

"Does this mean I'm going to have to give Cree his vial of blood back?" Macie asked.

He should've been surprised at her question, but it was only one of the things that made Macie so unique and impossible to resist. "Only if you agree to marry me."

"In that case." She dipped her hand into her slacks

pocket and pulled a necklace with what looked like an actual vial of blood hanging from the middle. "I'm not going to need this anymore." She tossed the vial at Gregson and launched herself down into Riggs's arms.

The momentum knocked his bum leg off-balance, and they toppled to the floor. Hoots and hollers exploded throughout the living room, followed by a handful of clapping as Macie pressed her mouth to his.

This was it. Everything he'd wanted since he'd been ten years old and in love with a girl way out of his league.

And it'd only taken about twenty-five years and a serial killer to get to her.

* * * * *

COMING NEXT MONTH FROM

H HARLEQUIN

INTRIGUE

#2151 TARGETED IN SILVER CREEK
Silver Creek Lawmen: Second Generation • by Delores Fossen
A horrific shooting left pregnant artist Hanna Kendrick with no memory of
Deputy Jesse Ryland...nor the night their newborn son was conceived. But
when the gunman escapes prison and places Hannah back in his crosshairs,
only Jesse can keep his child and the woman he loves safe.

#2152 DISAPPEARANCE IN DREAD HOLLOW
Lookout Mountain Mysteries • by Debra Webb
A crime spree has rocked Sheriff Tara Norwood's quiet town. Her only lead
is a missing couple's young son...and the teacher he trusts. Deke Shepherd
vows to aid his ex's investigation and protect the boy. But when life-threatening
danger and unresolved romance collide, will the stakes be too high?

#2153 CONARD COUNTY: CODE ADAM
Conard County: The Next Generation • by Rachel Lee
Big city detective Valerie Brighton will risk everything to locate her
kidnapped niece. Even partner with lawman Guy Redwing, despite
reservations about his small-town detective skills. But with bullets flying and
time running out, Guy proves he's the only man capable of saving a child's
life...and Valerie's jaded heart.

#2154 THE EVIDENCE NEXT DOOR
Kansas City Crime Lab • by Julie Miller
Wounded warrior Grayson Malone has become the KCPD's most brilliant
criminologist. When his neighbor Allie Tate is targeted by a stalker, he doesn't
hesitate to help. But soon the threats take a terrorizing, psychological toll.
And Grayson must provide answers *and* protection to keep her alive.

#2155 OZARKS WITNESS PROTECTION
Arkansas Special Agents • by Maggie Wells
Targeted by her husband's killer, pregnant widow and heiress Kayla Powers
needs a protection plan—pronto. But 24/7 bodyguard duty challenges
Special Agent Ryan Hastings's security skills...and professional boundaries.
Then Kayla volunteers herself as bait to bring the elusive assassin to justice...

#2156 HUNTING A HOMETOWN KILLER
Shield of Honor • by *Shelly Bell*
FBI Special Agent Rhys Keller has tracked a serial killer to his small
mountain hometown—and Julia Harcourt's front door. Safeguarding his
world-renowned ex in close quarters resurrects long buried emotions. But
will their unexpected reunion end in the murderer's demise...or theirs?

YOU CAN FIND MORE INFORMATION ON UPCOMING HARLEQUIN TITLES,
FREE EXCERPTS AND MORE AT HARLEQUIN.COM.

HICNM0523

Get 4 FREE REWARDS!

We'll send you 2 FREE Books plus 2 FREE Mystery Gifts.

FREE Value Over **$20**

Both the **Harlequin Intrigue®** and **Harlequin® Romantic Suspense** series feature compelling novels filled with heart-racing action-packed romance that will keep you on the edge of your seat.

YES! Please send me 2 FREE novels from the Harlequin Intrigue or Harlequin Romantic Suspense series and my 2 FREE gifts (gifts are worth about $10 retail). After receiving them, if I don't wish to receive any more books, I can return the shipping statement marked "cancel." If I don't cancel, I will receive 6 brand-new Harlequin Intrigue Larger-Print books every month and be billed just $6.49 each in the U.S. or $6.99 each in Canada, a savings of at least 13% off the cover price, or 4 brand-new Harlequin Romantic Suspense books every month and be billed just $5.49 each in the U.S. or $6.24 each in Canada, a savings of at least 12% off the cover price. It's quite a bargain! Shipping and handling is just 50¢ per book in the U.S. and $1.25 per book in Canada.* I understand that accepting the 2 free books and gifts places me under no obligation to buy anything. I can always return a shipment and cancel at any time by calling the number below. The free books and gifts are mine to keep no matter what I decide.

Choose one: ☐ **Harlequin Intrigue Larger-Print** (199/399 HDN GRJK) ☐ **Harlequin Romantic Suspense** (240/340 HDN GRJK)

Name (please print)

Address   Apt. #

City   State/Province   Zip/Postal Code

Email: Please check this box ☐ if you would like to receive newsletters and promotional emails from Harlequin Enterprises ULC and its affiliates. You can unsubscribe anytime.

Mail to the **Harlequin Reader Service:**
IN U.S.A.: P.O. Box 1341, Buffalo, NY 14240-8531
IN CANADA: P.O. Box 603, Fort Erie, Ontario L2A 5X3

Want to try 2 free books from another series! Call 1-800-873-8635 or visit www.ReaderService.com.

*Terms and prices subject to change without notice. Prices do not include sales taxes, which will be charged (if applicable) based on your state or country of residence. Canadian residents will be charged applicable taxes. Offer not valid in Quebec. This offer is limited to one order per household. Books received may not be as shown. Not valid for current subscribers to the Harlequin Intrigue or Harlequin Romantic Suspense series. All orders subject to approval. Credit or debit balances in a customer's account(s) may be offset by any other outstanding balance owed by or to the customer. Please allow 4 to 6 weeks for delivery. Offer available while quantities last.

Your Privacy—Your information is being collected by Harlequin Enterprises ULC, operating as Harlequin Reader Service. For a complete summary of the information we collect, how we use this information and to whom it is disclosed, please visit our privacy notice located at corporate.harlequin.com/privacy-notice. From time to time we may also exchange your personal information with reputable third parties. If you wish to opt out of this sharing of your personal information, please visit readerservice.com/consumerschoice or call 1-800-873-8635. **Notice to California Residents**—Under California law, you have specific rights to control and access your data. For more information on these rights and how to exercise them, visit corporate.harlequin.com/california-privacy.

HIHRS22R3

HARLEQUIN
PLUS

Try the best multimedia
subscription service for romance
readers like you!

Read, Watch and Play.

Experience the easiest way to get
the romance content you crave.

Start your **FREE TRIAL** at
<u>www.harlequinplus.com/freetrial</u>.

HARPLUS0123